Heidi Rice

THE CEO'S IMPOSSIBLE HEIR

Recycling programs
for this product may
not exist in your area.

ISBN-13: 978-1-335-56932-5

The CEO's Impossible Heir

Copyright © 2022 by Heidi Rice

This edition published by arrangement with Harlequin Books S.A.

For questions and comments about the quality of this book,
please contact us at CustomerService@Harlequin.com.

Harlequin Enterprises ULC
22 Adelaide St. West, 41st Floor
Toronto, Ontario M5H 4E3, Canada
www.Harlequin.com

Printed in U.S.A.

USA TODAY bestselling author **Heidi Rice** lives in London, England. She is married with two teenage sons—which gives her rather too much of an insight into the male psyche—and also works as a film journalist. She adores her job, which involves getting swept up in a world of high emotions; sensual excitement; funny, feisty women; sexy, tortured men; and glamorous locations where laundry doesn't exist. Once she turns off her computer, she often does chores—usually involving laundry!

Books by Heidi Rice

Harlequin Presents

A Forbidden Night with the Housekeeper
Innocent's Desert Wedding Contract

Hot Summer Nights with a Billionaire

One Wild Night with Her Enemy

Passion in Paradise

My Shocking Monte Carlo Confession

The Christmas Princess Swap

The Royal Pregnancy Test

Secrets of Billionaire Siblings

The Billionaire's Proposition in Paris

Visit the Author Profile page
at Harlequin.com for more titles.

To my dad, Peter Rice, where my love of
Ireland—and Irish heroes—began.

CHAPTER ONE

ROSS DE COURTNEY STRODE into the ancient chapel, having landed his helicopter five minutes ago on a clifftop on the west coast of Ireland.

The chapel was nestled in the grounds of his soon-to-be new brother-in-law's imposing estate—and currently decorated in glowing lights and scented winter blooms, and packed with a crowd full of people he did not know.

Soon-to-be, my arse.

A few of the assembled guests glanced his way as he headed down the aisle towards the happy couple who were in the midst of saying their vows—the groom dressed in a slate-grey designer suit and the bride, Ross's foolishly sweet and trusting sister, Katie, in a flowing white concoction of silk and lace.

His footsteps echoed on the old stone but were silenced by the thuds of his own heartbeat and the fury squeezing his chest.

Katie had asked him—very politely—in a message yesterday not to attend the ceremony.

It was the first time she'd deigned to return any of his calls or messages for months. She had 'things to tell him' apparently—important things that needed tact and delicacy to convey—about her newly acquired fiancé, the Irish billionaire Conall O'Riordan who Ross had met exactly once, five months ago now, at the opera in London.

Tact and delicacy, my arse.

The man was a thug, a ruthless, controlling thug who, just like the first man Katie had married—when she was just nineteen and the boy had only a few weeks to live—was not nearly good enough for her.

He'd done the wrong thing, then. Objecting to Katie's foolish decision to marry Tom and then standing back and waiting for her to see reason. And of course she hadn't, because Katie was a romantic. So she'd gone ahead and married Tom. Tom had died, and Ross and Katie hadn't spoken for five years, until that fortuitous night at the opera in December. When her Irish fiancé—who Ross did not know from Adam—had all but attacked him.

Well, he wasn't making the same mistake twice. This time he refused to see his sister hitch herself to another man who might hurt her.

Maybe he had no right to intervene in her life. She was twenty-four now, not nineteen. And the truth was, he'd never been much of a brother to her… Mostly because he'd never even known of his half-sister's existence until she was fourteen and her mother—one of his father's many discarded mistresses—had died. He'd tried to do the right thing then, paying for expensive schools and then college and publicly acknowledging her connection to the De Courtney family. Something his father in his usual cruel and selfish way had resolutely refused to do while he was still alive.

Even though they'd never been close, he couldn't let her marry O'Riordan, without at least making his feelings known.

More heads turned towards him as he approached the altar, the words of the ceremony barely audible above the thunder in his ears.

Personally, he would not have chosen to do this on the day, at the ceremony, like some scene straight out of a gothic novel or a Hollywood movie. But Katie had left him with no choice. She hadn't replied in any detail to the texts and emails he'd sent her trying to re-establish contact after their disastrous reunion at the opera five months ago. Her insistence she was going ahead with this wedding because she was madly in love with O'Riordan hadn't reassured him in the least.

Had the man cast some kind of a spell over his sister, with his money and his looks—or worse, was he a man like their father, who exerted a ruthless control over the women in his life?

The ceremony was reaching its peak when a young woman caught his eye, standing to the right of the groom holding the hand of a little boy dressed in a miniature suit.

Her wild red hair was piled on top of her head and threaded through with wild flowers.

The shot of heat and adrenaline and recognition that blasted into him was so fierce his steps faltered—and for one hideous moment he was back at the Westmoreland Summer Ball four years ago, dancing with the beautiful woman who had enchanted and mesmerised him that night.

Is it her?

He couldn't see her face, just her back, her bare shoulders, the graceful line of her neck, the seductive curve of one breast, the slender waist and long legs. He dragged his gaze back up, and it snagged on her nape again, the pale skin accentuated by the tendrils curling down from her hairdo.

He shook his head, tried to focus, the heat so real and all-consuming it momentarily obliterated his common sense.

Don't be ridiculous. It can't be her. This is your memory playing nasty tricks on you at a time of heightened emotion, which is precisely why you avoid this kind of drama, wherever possible.

The girl, whose name he'd never even known, had captivated him that night. Her quick, caustic wit delivered in a musical Irish accent and her bright, ethereal beauty—all flowing russet hair, translucent skin and piercing blue eyes—had momentarily turned him into an intoxicated and rapacious fool.

The heat kicked him squarely in the crotch as he recalled what had happened later that night, in the estate's garden. The fairy lights had cast a twinkle of magic over her soft skin as he'd devoured her. The subtle scent of night jasmine and ripe apples had been overwhelmed by the potent scent of her arousal as he'd stroked the slick heart of her desire. Her shattered sobs of pleasure had driven him wild as he'd eventually plunged into her and ridden them both towards oblivion...

They'd ended up making love—or rather having raw, sweaty, no-holds-barred sex—against an apple tree, not thirty yards from the rest of the party.

But what had seemed hopelessly hot and even weirdly romantic—given that he was not a romantic man—had turned first into an embarrassing obsession... After she'd run off—deliberately creating some kind of hokey Cinderella fantasy, he'd realised later—and he'd searched for her like a madman… And had then hit the cold, hard wall of reality three weeks later, when she'd contacted him on a withheld number, believing she could extort money out of him with the calculated lie he had got her pregnant.

And thus had ended his hot Cinderella fantasy.

Except it hadn't quite, because he still thought about her far too much. And, damn it, still had this visceral reaction when he spotted random women in crowds who had similar colouring or tilted their heads in a similar way. It was mortifying and infuriating, and seriously inconvenient. How typical he should be struck down by that deranged response now, when it could cause him maximum damage.

'If any man or woman knows of any lawful impediment why these two should not be joined in holy matrimony, speak now or for ever hold your peace.'

The priest's voice rang out, jolting Ross out of the memories and slamming him back into reality.

He dragged his gaze away from the offending bridesmaid's neck and forced the heat in his groin into a box marked 'get over yourself'.

He stood for a second, suspended in time, furious at being forced into such a public display, but at the same time knowing he could not let this moment—however clichéd—pass. Katie had left him with no choice.

'I object,' he said. And watched Katie and the mad Irishman swing round.

Gasps echoed throughout the crowd. And Katie's eyes widened. 'Ross? What are you doing here?'

Her groom's brows drew down in a furious frown. One Ross recognised from five long months ago at the opera the first time the man had laid eyes on him. The concern for his sister's welfare, which had been twisting his gut in knots for seven hours during the flight across the Atlantic, turned to stone.

You think I give a damn about your temper, buddy? No way am I letting you marry her until I know for sure you're not going to hurt her.

'What am I doing here?' he said, as conversationally as he could while the concern and the fury began to strangle him. 'I'm stopping this wedding until I can be sure this is what you really want, Katie,' he said, glad clarity had returned to his thoughts after the nasty little trick his memory had played on him.

But then the strangest thing happened: instead of saying anything, both Katie and her Irish groom turned to their left—ignoring him.

'Carmel, I'm so sorry,' his sister whispered.

'Mel, take Mac out of here,' the madman said in a voice that brooked no argument.

But then Ross turned too, realising the comments were directed at the young woman he had spotted a few moments before.

Recognition slammed into him like a freight train.

Her fierce blue eyes sparkled like sapphires—sheened with astonishment. The vibrant red hair only accentuated the flush racing over her pale features… And stabbed him hard in the chest.

The heat raced back, swiftly followed by a wave of shock. The concern that had been building inside him for hours now, ever since he'd made the decision to fly across the Atlantic, then pilot a helicopter to this godforsaken estate in the middle of nowhere to protect his sister, turned to something raw and painful.

It is her.

'Mammy, who's yer man?'

Ross's gaze dipped to the little boy standing beside her. The childish voice, tinged with the soft lilt of the boy's homeland, cut through the adult storm gathering around them.

The shock twisted in his stomach and his heartbeat slowed, the emotions rising in his chest becoming strangely opaque—almost as if he had walked into a fog and couldn't find his way out again. He took in the child's striking blue-green eyes, round with curiosity, his perfect little features, and the short blond curls rioting around his head, but all he could see was himself, aged about four, in the only picture he'd ever seen of himself as a child with his mother. Before his hair had darkened. And she had died. A photo his father had taken great pleasure in burning in front of him, when he was being sent off to boarding school.

'Stop snivelling, boy. Your mother was weak. You don't want to be weak too, do you?'

'What…?' The word choked out, barely audible as his gaze rose back to the woman's face, the horror engulfing him. 'How…?'

No. No. No.

This could not be true. This could not be happening. This was a dream. Not a dream. A waking nightmare.

He pressed his fingers to his temples, his gaze jerking between her and the child.

This toddler could not be his… His mind screamed in denial. He had taken the ultimate precaution to prevent this eventuality. He would not believe it.

She wrapped her arm around the boy's shoulders, to edge the child behind her and shield him from Ross's view.

'It's okay, Mac,' she said, the smoky voice he recognised edged now with anger but no less seductive—her stance defiant and brave as she straightened to her full height, like a young Valkyrie protecting her offspring. 'This man is nobody.'

He stepped towards her, determined to do… Something!

Who the hell are you kidding?

He had no clue what to do! The shock was still reverberating through him with such force, his sense of time and place and his usual cast-iron control had completely deserted him.

A strong hand on his shoulder dragged him back a step. 'Get away from my sister, you bastard.'

He recognised the madman's voice, could hear Katie's straight afterwards, begging them both to calm down, but all he could do was stand and stare as his hot Cinderella lifted the child into her arms and headed towards the vestry.

She's running away from me again.

For a moment he was back in the orchard, still struggling to deal with the shattering orgasm as he watched her panicked figure disappear into the moonlight.

But instead of scrambling to throw off the drugging afterglow while zipping up his trousers so he could charge after her, this time, he stood frozen to the spot. The boy's gaze met his as the child clung to his mother's neck. The neck that had driven him wild all those years ago… And again just moments before.

'You need to leave.' The groom tugged him round. 'You weren't invited and no one wants you here.'

'Take your hands off me,' he managed as he broke the man's hold.

He swung back. He had to follow her, and the boy, but his movements were stiff and mechanical. His racing heart punched his chest wall, the residual surge of heat—always there when he thought of her—only disturbing him more.

O'Riordan grabbed his arm this time. 'Come back here, you son of a...'

Ross turned, his fist clenched, ready to swat the bastard like a fly, but he couldn't seem to think coherently, or coordinate his body, so when he aimed at the man's head, he missed.

The answering blow shot towards him so fast he had no chance to evade it. Pain exploded in his jaw, his head snapping back.

The fog darkened.

'That's an impressive right hook,' he murmured, holding his burning face, a metallic taste filling his mouth as he staggered backwards.

The cries of assorted guests and Katie's tear-streaked face were the last things he was aware of as he collapsed into an oddly welcome oblivion.

But as he dropped into the abyss, one last coherent thought tortured him.

How can she have given me a child...when I can never be anyone's father?

CHAPTER TWO

'GET OUT OF *my way. You said yourself there are no signs of a concussion, so I would like to leave now.*'

'*But Mr De Courtney, I think it's best if you rest a while. You're clearly exhausted.*'

'*I'm not staying.*'

Carmel O'Riordan stood in the hallway of Kildaragh Castle's east wing, stricken by the buzz in her abdomen at the sound of that deep, authoritative voice as Ross De Courtney argued with the paramedic Con had called after their uninvited wedding guest had been carried to this bedroom on the second floor.

She sank back against the wall, eavesdropping on the conversation, and tried to get up the guts to walk into the room... And confront her past.

The wedding had gone ahead, and now the reception was in full swing downstairs. But she still hadn't got over the shock of seeing Ross De Courtney again. Or discovering that Mac's father—a man whose identity she had never revealed to anyone, least of all her brother Conall—was also her new sister-in-law's brother.

She pressed damp palms to the thin silk of her bridesmaid's dress. Her fingers were shaking, because she couldn't get the picture out of her head of Ross's face, those sharp iridescent blue-green eyes going wide with surprise then dazed with shock as he'd looked upon her son— *their* son—for the first time twenty minutes ago.

Would that memory be lodged in her brain now for all eternity? Like all the others that had derailed her so many times in the last four years?

The sight of Ross De Courtney—tall and debonair in a dark tuxedo illuminated by the soft glow of torch light in an apple orchard, his gaze locked on hers, his touch tender and yet insatiable. His scent musky and addictive. His voice low with command and thick with desire. Each recollection gilded by the devastating heat and the wayward emotions that had intoxicated her.

She'd been such a fool that night, having gatecrashed Westmoreland's famous ball on the outskirts of London with her college friend Cheryl. All the way there in the car Cheryl had borrowed, they'd been busy joking about finding a billionaire to marry.

But then the joke had turned on her.

Ross De Courtney had been so handsome, so hot, so sophisticated and so into her—enjoying her bolshy sense of humour, never taking his eyes off her... He'd made her feel special and so, so grown up. After years of being desperate to feel like a woman instead of a girl, and finally get away from her brother Conall's overprotective custody, it had been so easy to believe it had all been real... Instead of a trick of the sultry summer night, her idiotic naiveté and her hyperactive hormones, which had homed in on him the minute she'd walked into the party and seen him standing alone. Ross had been moody and intense and hopelessly exciting—like Heathcliff and Mr Darcy and that vampire fella from *Twilight* all rolled into one.

She could still feel his touch on her skin, that sure, urgent excitement that had flowed through her like an electric current and made her do stupid things.

But then she'd run away, like an immature little fool. And hadn't even given a thought to protection until three weeks later, when her period had failed to arrive.

'Now where the hell are my shoes?'

The brittle words from inside the room cut through Carmel's brutal trip down memory lane.

She swallowed around the lump forming in her throat and curled her fingers into fists to stop them shaking. She couldn't stand in the hallway for ever. She needed to face this man. Truth was, she probably didn't have that long before Conall came barging up the stairs to 'protect' her. Katie might have an amazing effect on her brother, but even she wasn't going to be able to hold him back for ever when he was in 'mother bear' mode.

Her brother had crossed so many lines. He'd hired a damn private detective to discover the identity of the man she had always refused to name. When he'd discovered Ross De Courtney was Mac's daddy, he'd then hired Ross's sister Katie as an event planner for their sister Imelda's wedding to her childhood sweetheart, Donal, in December. But he'd never really intended for Katie to plan a wedding. What he'd *really* been about was finding a way to get vengeance on the man who had fathered her son. A vengeance Carmel had never asked for and Conall had no right to claim.

But then, instead of getting vengeance on Ross, Conall had fallen in love with Katie. And now Ross was integrated into her and Mac's lives—for ever—by virtue of his relationship to Conall's new wife.

The fact that neither Con nor Katie had thought to tell her any of this before *their* wedding had infuriated her downstairs. But now all she felt was numb. And scared.

Ross De Courtney had rejected Mac before

he was even born. Had accused her of lying about the pregnancy in a single damning text—the shock of which had taken her years to overcome. But she'd never forgotten a single word of his cruel instant reply after she'd worked up the courage to inform him of her pregnancy.

If you're pregnant, the child isn't mine. So if this is an attempt to extort money from me you're all out of luck.

How was she going to protect Mac from that rejection now? When Ross De Courtney was so closely related to her brother's wife?

But he hadn't looked dismissive or angry twenty minutes ago when he'd first set eyes on Mac. He'd looked absolutely stunned.

She needed to get to the bottom of that look, because it made no sense. Not only that, but that devastating text didn't make quite so much sense now either.

He'd accused her of terrible things, it was true, things she hadn't done. But there was no mistaking, she had come on to him that night.

He hadn't stolen her innocence, as her brother Conall liked to assume. She'd offered it to him, willingly.

She'd flirted with him mercilessly. She'd revelled in the role of virgin temptress and the way he'd made her feel. But as soon as the afterglow had faded, and the emotional impact had come crashing in on her, she'd run—like the little girl she was.

Virgin temptress, my butt. Virgin eejit more like.

All of which left enough grey areas now to make her question the conclusions she'd drawn about her child's father. What if he wasn't the out-and-out villain she'd assumed him to be? Whatever way she looked at it, the man was Mac's father. Had she been a coward to avoid addressing that reality in the years since? Coasting along on the assumption he didn't want to know his son thanks to one text. What if he had genuinely believed Mac wasn't his? She hadn't even considered that possibility before. Had simply assumed he'd wanted to be rid of her, hadn't wanted to live up to his responsibilities and had found the cruellest possible way to dump her and forget about that night.

But what if the truth were more complicated?

She tapped her clenched fist against the door. 'Can I come in?' she said, steeling herself against the inevitable reaction as she stepped into the room, without waiting for a reply.

She hadn't steeled herself enough.

Sensation blindsided her as Ross De Courtney's head turned, and those vivid eyes fixed on her face. She took in his dishevelled appearance—the half-open shirt speckled with blood revealing a tantalising glimpse of chest hair, the scuffed trousers, the shoeless feet, the roughened chestnut hair furrowed into haphazard rows, and the darkening bruise on his jaw.

She drew in a sharp breath to reinflate her lungs.

How could the man look even more gorgeous now than he had that night? How was that fair?

He didn't say anything, he simply stared at her, the harsh line of his lips flattening. There was no antagonism there, but neither was there welcome. And it occurred to her for the first time that, however incredible their one night together had been—and it *had* been incredible—Ross De Courtney had always been impossible to read.

He'd been focussed solely on her that night, but she'd never for a moment known what he was thinking. And that disturbed her even more now.

'Ms O'Riordan, perhaps you can talk some sense into my patient.' The middle-aged paramedic who stood beside Ross spoke and she noticed him for the first time. 'I believe Mr De Courtney should rest a bit…'

'It's okay…um… Joe, is it?' she said, gathering enough of her wits about her to read the poor harassed paramedic's name badge. 'You can leave us. If Mr De Courtney shows any signs of blacking out again, I'll call you immediately.'

The older man glanced at his reluctant patient, then nodded. 'Fine, I'll be leaving you to it, then.'

The door closed behind him with a dull thud, which reverberated in her chest.

Was she the only one who could feel the awareness crackling in the air like an electrical force field? The last time they'd been alone together, she'd still been struggling to cope with the after-effects of an orgasm so intense she was sure she must have passed out herself for a moment.

An orgasm from an encounter that had produced the most precious thing in her life.

The significance of that now though, and the fact she could still feel the residual heat from that encounter so long ago, only increased her fear. She clamped down on the agonising swell of sensation and the tangle of nerves in her gut as she held out her hand to indicate one of the suite's armchairs. A hand she was pleased to see trembled only slightly.

'Do you want to take a seat, Mr De Courtney?' she said, drawing on every last ounce of her composure to maintain some semblance of dignity.

'*Mr* De Courtney?' he said, his tone more sharp than surprised. '*Really?*'

'I'm trying to be polite,' she snapped as the strain took its toll.

Seriously? Did he want to make this even tougher than it was already?

'Why?' he asked, as if he really didn't know.

'Because my mammy insisted upon manners at all times, and I'm trying to live by her example,' she snapped back, because an inane question deserved an inane answer. 'Don't be an *eejit*. Why do you think?'

'I don't know,' he said, looking a lot more composed than she felt. 'That's why I asked.'

'Okay, then, if you want plain speaking it's because polite seemed preferable to punching you on the jaw again,' she said, even though it wasn't aggression she felt towards him but something much more confusing.

There were a myriad emotions running through her, and not one of them was as simple as anger. Unfortunately.

He looked away, then tugged his fingers through his hair. 'I wouldn't blame you if you did,' he murmured, the resignation as clear as the frustration.

'Why would you say that?' she asked, far too aware of the livid bruise spreading across his jaw. 'Con shouldn't have hit you. He had no right.'

However confusing her emotions were towards this man, she had a new appreciation of him now after asking his sister Katie downstairs if she thought her brother was a bad man… Because she had needed to know his sister's opinion before she confronted him.

And Katie's reply, while angering Conall—who had decided Ross De Courtney was a villain of the first order—had been a lot more nuanced. Apparently she and Ross had been estranged for five years—after her marriage to her first husband, which Ross hadn't approved of. But she had pointed out he had acknowledged her as a teenager as soon as he discovered her existence and paid for a string of expensive schools and governesses. So, although they had never been close, it had surprised Katie when Conall told her that Ross had refused to acknowledge Mac.

Ross had come to Kildaragh to stop the wedding. Carmel had no idea why exactly but, given the obvious animosity between him and Conall as soon as he had appeared, she suspected it stemmed from some misguided desire to protect his sister from a marriage to her brother. The man had no knowledge of why her brother had reacted so aggressively towards him all those months ago when they first met, so that much at least made some sort of sense.

'He had every right,' Ross said, as his gaze locked back on hers. He searched her face, sending that disconcerting heat through her again. 'He's your brother.'

'That's madness,' she said, suddenly a little tired of the big brothers' code of honour.

What gave men the right to make decisions about the women in their lives? And wasn't it beyond ironic he should support Conall's Neanderthal behaviour—given that he appeared to have come to Ireland to protect his sister from the same. 'Con did not have the right to interfere in my—'

'Is the boy mine?' he cut into her diatribe, slicing right through her indignation to the tender heart of the matter.

It hurt her to realise he didn't sound happy at the prospect, merely resigned.

She straightened.

'Yes, Mac is your son,' she said, refusing to be cowed by his underwhelming reaction.

Mac was the best thing to have happened to her, ever. A sweet, kind, funny, brave and bold little fella who was so much more than just someone's son. Maybe this man didn't feel the same way about him. But then he didn't know him… And, she had realised in the last hour, she had to take some of the responsibility for that. 'We can do a DNA test if you still don't believe me,' she snapped.

'That won't be necessary,' he said, taking the offer at face value and apparently unconcerned by the caustic tone. 'He looks just as I did at that age.'

He sat down heavily in the chair she had indicated. Not sat, so much as collapsed, as if all the breath had been yanked out of his lungs. He ran his fingers through his hair again, scraping it back from his forehead.

She noticed the exhaustion for the first time, in the bruised smudges beneath his eyes, the slumped line of his broad shoulders. And despite the anger she wanted to feel towards him, all she could feel in that moment was pity.

Because he didn't look resigned any more, he looked shattered.

She took the seat across from him, her legs shaky now too. She thought she'd been prepared to deal with this rejection again. Might even have hoped for it, as she made her way up to the suite, with every possible outcome from this meeting bouncing through her brain. Did she really want to allow Ross De Courtney a role in Mac's life? Wouldn't it be better if he didn't want to be Mac's father? Had no interest in getting to know him? Then she wouldn't have to deal with all the messy emotions of forming a relationship with a man who had devastated her once already. Or figure out if he should be a part of Mac's life. Because no matter whether he was Mac's biological father, that didn't give him any rights, in her opinion, unless she decided he was worthy of that place.

Wouldn't it be much easier not to have to make any of those decisions? To just go on as before?

But somehow, seeing his reaction, all she felt was devastated that he had no concept of how precious Mac was.

'Why were you so convinced I was lying,' she asked, attempting to keep her thoughts on Mac—and what was best for him, 'when I texted you?'

His head rose and she saw something flash in his gaze before he masked it. Regret? Sadness? Pain? It was impossible to tell.

He stared back at his hands, now clasped in his lap. His shoulders tightened into a rigid line. And she sensed the battle being waged. He didn't want to answer her question. But then he scrubbed his open palms down his face, cursed softly under his breath and straightened. The look he sent her was both direct and dispassionate.

'I did not believe the boy could possibly be mine, because I had myself sterilised, a decade ago, when I was twenty-one years old to avoid this ever happening.'

'You… What? But… *Why?*'

Ross could see the horror on Carmel O'Riordan's face. A face that had haunted his dreams for years, but, now it was in front of him, caused so many mixed emotions. All of them so far outside his comfort zone he was struggling to think with any clarity whatsoever.

She looked radiant, he thought, grimly. That vibrant russet hair, lit by the sunlight coming through the castle's casement windows, which made the red and gold tones even more vivid than they had been that night. Her pale skin was sprinkled with freckles he hadn't noticed four years ago in the moonlight. Had she covered them with make-up?

'Why would you do such a thing at such a young age?' she asked again.

He dragged his gaze away from her beauty. He'd fallen under that spell once before, and it had led them both here.

'A lot of reasons,' he said. Reasons he had no intention of elaborating on. He hadn't even wanted to tell her of the procedure he'd had done as soon as he could convince a doctor he knew what he was doing. But he figured he owed her the truth, to explain—if not condone—the mistakes he'd made four years ago. 'Anyway, my reasons are irrelevant now, because the procedure obviously didn't work.'

Once he got back to New York, he would have himself properly checked out. He'd never done any of the follow-up appointments. At the time he'd told himself he was far too busy, dealing with taking over the reins of De Courtney's and trying to drag it into the twenty-first century after his father's death. But looking back now, he could admit he'd found the constant prodding and poking emasculating—which would be ironic if it weren't so pathetic. He'd made the decision he did not ever want to get a woman pregnant, but he'd seen no need to dwell on it. He'd been a young man after all, foolish and impulsive and arrogant. As long as he could still get an erection, he had been more than happy after the effects of the operation had worn off.

And now he was a father. Responsible for another human life, who shared his DNA, and who would carry on the De Courtney line whether he wished it to be carried on or not. Although even that seemed a total irrelevance now. The reasons he'd based his decision on so long ago were all completely beside the point now that a little boy existed with his face and his blood...

'You don't...' He looked up to see her already pale skin had become ashen. 'You don't have some kind of genetic disease, do you? That you didn't want to pass on?'

'No.' *At least, not a biological one.*

'Oh, thank goodness.' Her shoulders slumped with relief. And he realised she had been terrified for her son. He waited for her to repeat her question about why he'd done it, but she surprised him. 'Do you think you might have other children you don't know about?'

The tremulous question, delivered in a gentle whisper, forced him to engage again, and answer her, when the thing he most wanted to do was disengage.

It had always been so much easier to deny his demons even existed, and now he was going to be forced to face them by a woman who could turn his insides to molten lava with a single breathless look.

The heat swelled and glowed in his abdomen, as it had an hour ago, when he'd got fixated on the back of her neck.

What was that even about? How could he still want her, when she had just turned his life upside down and inside out?

Nice try, you bastard. It wasn't her that did this, you did it to yourself. By being an arrogant, careless, entitled idiot who thought he could control his own fate.

'No,' he murmured. 'There won't be any others. You're the only woman I've ever had unprotected sex with,' he added, then stared back at his hands, aware of the pulsing ache in his jaw from her brother's punch as he clenched his teeth against the tidal wave of shame.

Exactly how desperate had he been to have her that night? Why hadn't he observed any of the danger signs, when he'd become so enchanted, so mesmerised, so addicted to her sultry smoky laugh, her quick wit and irreverent humour, that soft melodic accent, the earthy scent of her arousal?

Carmel O'Riordan was a stunning woman. Even more beautiful now than she had been then—but what the heck had got into him that night to make him forget every one of his own rules? And so quickly? Why had he been focussed solely on the need to plunge into her, to claim her, brand her, make her his? Because his behaviour had been nothing short of deranged, and he was very much afraid he still hadn't got a good firm grip on his attraction to her even now.

'Well, I guess that's good to know,' she said.

She brushed the tendrils back from her face, the nervous gesture oddly endearing.

He unlocked his jaw, to say what he should have said as soon as she came in.

'I owe you an apology, for that text,' he said. 'It was unforgivable.' He threaded his fingers through his hair for about the five thousandth time that day gathering the courage to get it all out. 'And I owe your brother an apology too.'

Her brows launched up her forehead. 'Why on earth would you owe Con an apology?'

'I came here today to talk some sense into my sister, convinced Conall O'Riordan was a violent, volatile, controlling man who might do her harm, based on our one chance meeting in London months ago. I'm guessing now that at the time we met at the opera he already knew my connection to you, and his nephew?'

She nodded. 'Yes, apparently he did, he hired

a private detective to find out your identity after I refused to tell him who you were. The arrogant—'

'I see,' he said, to halt her insults, not sure why the fact she hadn't divulged his name all those years ago should make the ache in his jaw move into his ribcage.

Why hadn't she told O'Riordan who he was when she found herself pregnant and alone? And why hadn't she ever followed up that text to demand a DNA test? All this time she had been surviving without any support from him… And okay, perhaps she didn't need his financial support—after all, her brother was a wealthy man—but still, the child had always been his responsibility, not her brother's. No wonder the man had looked as if he wanted to castrate him all those months ago in London. He'd had good cause.

'It doesn't matter how your brother discovered my identity,' he continued, rubbing the spot on his chest where the ache had centred.

He'd spent his whole life, determined not to be like his father, not to be as cruel or callous or controlling. Ross had prided himself on always keeping things light and non-committal with women, which was why his reaction to Carmel O'Riordan had bothered him so much. But he could see now how low he'd set the bar for himself, and with that text to Carmel—when she had informed him of her pregnancy—he'd failed to rise even to that pitiful level.

'The way your brother spoke to me that evening was not unprovoked as I had assumed. Nor was it born of a desire to isolate or control my sister's associations with me. Instead, he was motivated by a desire to protect you from a man he knew had wronged you, terribly.' He cringed inwardly. Good lord, the ironies just kept piling up. 'Which makes my presence here—and my attempt to interfere in your brother's marriage to my sister—wrong on every level.'

He stood and grabbed his jacket off the bed, the battle to maintain a semblance of control and ignore the claustrophobic weight starting to crush his ribs all but impossible. He needed time and space to deal with the emotions still churning inside him. Only then would he be able to figure out the best way to make amends, to her and her family and the boy. 'Which is my cue to leave, hopefully with more dignity than when I arrived,' he said. 'Although that could be a problem as I can't locate my shoes,' he added, the pathetic attempt at humour falling flat when her huge blue eyes widened and her brows rose further up her forehead. 'Perhaps you could speak to the paramedic and find out where he put them?'

'Wait a minute…' Carmel leapt to her feet—and placed her hands on her hips in a stubborn stance that accentuated her stunning figure in the slinky bridesmaid's dress.

The ache sank into his abdomen. *Great.*

'You're leaving?' she demanded. 'Just like that? Are you mad?' she said, her accent thickening.

Why did that fiery outrage only make her more irresistible? When he'd never been a man to appreciate any form of discord. Especially not with women he was dating… Not that he was dating her, he reminded himself, forcefully.

'What about Cormac?' she said.

'Who's Cormac?' he asked.

'Your son,' she snapped back with all the passion he could see sparking in her eyes.

Yes, of course.

He frowned, wondering how he had managed to forget about the huge elephant in the room, which was now pressing down on his chest again like a ten-ton weight. Score two to the heat pulsing in his pants. Yet more reason to be exceptionally wary of it.

'My legal team will be in touch as soon as I return to New York,' he said, determined to be as fair as he could be.

There was no way to repay her for what he had done, but he wanted to be as generous as possible. In fact, he would have to insist on it.

'If you'd like to make an accounting of your expenditure up to now, I will pay you the full amount…as I consider the error that resulted in your pregnancy to be mine. You can rest assured the maintenance I will pay for you and the boy going forward—and the trust fund I will set up for him—should ensure you and he will never want for anything ever again.'

CHAPTER THREE

AN ACCOUNTING? THE ERROR? What the actual...?

Carmel could feel her head exploding. She was so furious with the man in front of her, talking in that crisp, clear, completely passionless tone about her beautiful little boy—*their* beautiful little boy. Did he believe making an accounting of profit and loss would absolve him of his responsibilities as Mac's father? *Really?*

The outrage queued up in her throat like a stick of dynamite, stopping any coherent words from coming out of her mouth. She glared at him as he spotted his shoes under a chair and slipped them on, obviously intending to simply walk out of the door.

As he stepped past her she threw up her hands and slammed them against his chest, knocking him back a step. The ripple of reaction shot down her spine, at the flex of muscle and sinew, the whiff of his familiar scent—woodsy aftershave and soap—that got caught in her throat right beside the dynamite.

'Where do you think you're going?' she growled as the outrage exploded out of her mouth.

'Manhattan,' he offered.

'But you can't just go, this isn't over. I don't want an accounting. When did I ever ask you for money?' she shouted as her outrage grew like a wild beast.

She gripped his shirt front, far too conscious of the awareness in his eyes and the electric energy flowing between them as his muscles tensed.

'You didn't,' he said, still calm, still dispassionate, even though the fire in his gaze was telling her he was as affected by the contact as she was.

He gripped her wrists, disengaged her hands from his torn shirt, but the feel of his thumbs touching her thundering pulse points sent her senses into overdrive—only making her more mad.

'But that's hardly the point,' he added, letting her wrists go to step away from her, as if she were a bomb about to detonate. 'I owe you a considerable amount for the boy's upkeep.'

'The boy has a name. It's Mac, or Little Mac, or Cormac when he's being naughty and I have to get stern with him.' She was babbling, but it was the only way to keep the outrage and the hurt at bay.

He blinked, as if the information was a complete anathema to him. 'I see,' he said, but she knew he really didn't see. There was so much she wanted to tell him about his child. Did he really not want to know any of it?

'And he doesn't need your money. What he needs is a father.'

He stiffened then, and his jaw tensed, his expression guarded. But she could still see the fire in his eyes. 'I'm afraid I can't offer him that,' he said, still not saying their child's name. 'I'm not capable of being anyone's father, other than in a financial sense.'

Oh, for the love of...

She cursed under her breath, suddenly sick of his platitudes and evasions.

'How could you possibly know that if you've never even tried?' she asked, exasperated now as well as angry.

Why did he have himself sterilised as a young man?

He hadn't given her an explanation, clearly hadn't wanted to. But she found it hard to believe such a momentous decision could have been a frivolous one.

But still, he hadn't said he didn't *want* to be a father, he'd said he wasn't *capable* of being one. Which were two very different things. Maybe she was clutching at straws here, wanting to see more in him than was there. But there was a definite disconnect between a man who would fly thousands of miles to disrupt a wedding to save his sister from a man he believed might abuse her and the man who had barely spoken to the same sister in years. It made no sense. And Carmel had always been someone who had looked for sense in everything... Ever since her mother had taken her own life and everyone— her brother included—had resolutely refused to talk about it.

She hated secrets. She had always believed that talking about stuff openly and honestly was the only way to get to the heart of the matter and fix what was broken. Which was precisely why being unable to talk openly and honestly to her family, and more importantly her son, about his father over the last four years had been so damaging.

That ended now.

She had made mistakes too. Instead of allowing his one brutal text to make her a coward, and shielding her heart from more pain, she should have followed it up. Demanded to know why he had reacted so callously...

Well, she wasn't running any more.

'I don't need to try, when I know I won't be any good at it,' he said, through gritted teeth now, clearly holding onto his temper with an effort.

Good. Temper was better than the calm, controlled mask she'd been treated to so far—with his brittle apologies and his complete failure to explain his motivations. He was going to have to do a lot better than that before he'd be rid of her.

'How do you know?' she tried again.

'Because I just do,' he said, as stubborn as ever.

'Well, I don't believe that.' He'd never even met Mac, so how could he possibly know whether they would bond or not? But she didn't say as much. Because she had no intention of letting him bond with her precious child before she knew a lot more about him. But one thing she did know was that she was not about to let him buy off his paternal responsibilities as Mac's father either. The way he had clearly done with his fraternal responsibilities when he found out about his sister's existence. According to Katie, Ross had paid for expensive schools, tutors, governesses, even college, but he had never given her much of his time.

'No one knows if they'll be any good at parenthood until they have to do it,' she added. If all he felt right now towards Mac was responsibility, that was at least a start. Something they could work with. 'You have to learn on the job. Do you really think I thought I could be a mother at nineteen?'

His eyes widened and he winced. 'You were *nineteen* that night?' He ran his fingers through his hair, the blood draining out of his face. 'Good God, you were a child.'

'Nonsense,' she shot back.

He's worse than Conall. Men and their white knight complexes!

'I was a woman fully grown, with a woman's wants and needs…' Maybe she'd been naïve and foolish, and more than a little starstruck by him. But she'd known full well what she was doing and she'd enjoyed every second of it. Until the emotional consequences had hit home. 'And I believe I proved it rather comprehensively. As I recall, you were as well satisfied as I was that night,' she added, something about his concern making her feel like that reckless girl again. 'In fact, I should probably thank you,' she added, unable to stop herself from rubbing it in. 'I've heard tell from friends that a woman's first time is rarely as good as you made mine.'

'You were a virgin as well?' He hissed the words, shock turning to horror.

'Not for long,' she said, feeling like the badass she was when he cursed and slumped back into the chair.

Holding his head in his hands, he groaned. 'I'm surprised your brother didn't take out a contract on me after he found out my identity,' he said. 'Right now, I'd like to take one out on myself.'

The abject regret in his voice, the flags of

shameful colour on his tanned cheeks had her going with instinct and reaching out to touch his shoulder. 'There's no need to take on so over it,' she said. 'When I was the one who came on to you?'

Yes, she'd been a little younger than him and hopelessly inexperienced, but she'd wanted to lose her virginity that night. And it had been spectacular, so she had no regrets about that much.

'Did you?' he said, his brows flattening in a grim line.

The doubt in his tone should have annoyed her more. She'd known her own mind that night, and she refused to let him take that power away from her just because he'd been her first and she'd been younger than he thought. But his gallantry was also intriguing. For a man who professed to be incapable of parenthood, he seemed to have a strong moral code.

'I'm not sure you did,' he said. 'All I can remember is I wanted you more than I'd ever wanted any woman before as soon as I set eyes on you. Damn it, Carmel, I took you against a tree your first time. Without using protection and without properly checking how old you were. It sickens me to even think of it.'

'You asked me my age twice, and both times I lied,' she supplied, her heart pulsing strangely alongside the heat that refused to dim at the force in his statement.

'I wanted you more than I'd ever wanted any woman before as soon as I set eyes on you.'

So she *had* been special to him, at least in one respect. Good to know she wasn't the only one who had been blindsided by their physical chemistry.

'You did everything short of asking me for my ID,' she continued. 'As I had a very good fake one on me, even if you had, it wouldn't have done any good.'

'If I asked you twice, I must have suspected you weren't telling me the truth,' he said. 'Can't you see how wrong that is?'

'No, I can't.' She stood and strode across the room, suddenly needing to move, the pulsing at her core threatening to become as distracting now as it had been then.

It didn't matter if their chemistry was still strong, indulging it again was not an option. Not when their son would be caught in the middle. All of which meant talking about the events of that night—however satisfying she found it to goad him—probably was not a good idea, because it brought those needs and desires back into sharp focus.

She had a vibrator to quench that thirst now. She didn't need him. Or any man, and it would be best if she remembered that.

'But anyway, we're getting off the point,' she said, suddenly desperate to turn the conversation back to the matter at hand.

'What *was* the point exactly?' he asked.

'That I'm not going to let you give me or Mac any of your money.'

'What? That's preposterous.' He stood and crossed the room towards her. She held her ground, determined not to be swayed—even though she didn't know another man who wore righteous indignation as well.

Really, had he ever looked hotter? With his torn shirt and the stormy expression in those vivid aquamarine eyes finally making him look how she had always remembered him. Gone was the dispassionate control of moments ago, the brittle apology and the chilling cruelty of that text. This was the man she had met that night—exciting, forthright, determined and, oh, so passionate.

Okay, passion is so not the issue here, Mel.

Getting past that chilling control was what mattered, because she wanted to know him, not the masks he wore.

'On the contrary, we've just established how much I owe you,' he said. 'Not just for the child but also for what I did to you that night.'

The child? Why couldn't he say their son's name?

'In fairness, we've established no such thing,'

she pointed out. 'All we've established is that you have a white knight complex almost as over-developed as my brother's. And that you think you can rid yourself of your paternal responsibilities to Mac by putting them into a neat little box called expenses paid. Well, I'm telling you, you can't.'

'What the hell does that even mean? I'm the boy's father. I have a responsibility towards him. And to you for what I took from you that night.'

'And as I've told you just now, you took nothing from me that I was not willing to give. And you gave me the most precious thing in my life in return, so you can consider that column already paid off.'

'Stop being deliberately facetious.' He glared at her, his expression thunderous. 'That's not what I'm offering and you know it.'

Oh, yes, it is, Ross, why can't you see that?

She stifled the wave of sympathy at how emotionally obtuse he appeared to be. And went for the jugular.

'If you don't wish to have a relationship with Mac, I'll certainly not force you to have one. The last thing I want is a father for my son who isn't interested in being one.' She knew what that was like, because her own mother had struggled to bond with her and Imelda and even Con. It hadn't been her mother's fault. But that didn't alter the awful effect her mother's emotional neglect had had on her and her siblings.

Con had closed himself off to emotion, Imelda had become lost in her own fantasy world. And she'd become wild and difficult, and hopelessly self-destructive. Because buried deep in her subconscious had been the certainty there must have been something terribly wrong with her if her own mother couldn't love her. Of course, she had come to see more clearly, after becoming a mother herself, it was her mother's depression that had robbed them both of that crucial connection.

She would never willingly subject her son to the same neglect, if something similar afflicted Ross that he was unwilling or unable to address. But that said, there was enough that didn't add up to make her wonder if Ross *could* be a father despite his protestations…

'Then what are we even arguing about?' he asked, even more exasperated.

'Simply this. If you're not prepared to be a father to Cormac, you can leave now and never see or speak to him or me again. But if you do that, I will not allow you to give him money. No maintenance, no trust fund, no generous allowance. Mac needs a daddy, not a piggy bank. You can be both, or you can be neither. And that's my final word on it.'

'*Your* final word?' Ross had to clench his teeth to stop himself from yelling, so frustrated, and frankly furious, he would not have been surprised if actual steam had started pouring from his ears.

Good God, she was the most incorrigible, intractable and stubborn woman he'd ever met. So intractable she seemed determined to harm herself as well as her son's best interests simply to make some asinine point.

'Yes,' she said, her chin popping out as if she needed to reiterate said asinine point. 'Take it or leave it.'

Right now, what he'd like to do was kiss that stubborn pout off her lips until she...

He cut off the insane direction of his thoughts as the damning heat spread through his system like wildfire.

Great, he was actually losing his mind. It was official.

He turned his back on her and crossed the room to stare out of the window. The waves crashed onto the rocks below them, echoing his turbulent mood.

Terrific, even the damn landscape is mocking me now.

He dragged his fingers through his hair, trying to calm his breathing, and dowse the heat once and for all so he could think.

At this rate, I'll be lucky if I'm not bald by the end of today.

He shoved his hands into the pockets of his trousers, far too aware of her standing behind him, waiting for an answer.

Unfortunately, she had him over a barrel. Even if she didn't know it yet.

Because there was no way in hell he could simply walk away from this situation, now. Not with his sense of honour intact. Not after everything that had transpired four years ago—and his damning role in it. Because that really would make him as much of a monster as his father.

He'd destroyed Carmel O'Riordan's innocence four years ago.

Perhaps she had been willing and able to make her own decisions despite her youth and lack of experience... But he had exploited the physical connection between them ruthlessly, kissing and caressing her fragrant flesh in every place he knew would stoke her desire to fever pitch. That her artless, eager response had managed to set fire to his own libido—until he'd lost every ounce of his usual caution—was ultimately his responsibility too, because she'd had no idea at the time what she was doing to him.

To compound his crimes, he had then treated her appallingly with that knee-jerk text and there was also the boy to consider. A helpless, innocent child who hadn't chosen this situation. The only way he could live with himself was if he provided the boy—his son—with all the support he could ever need. Financially, at least.

So how did he persuade her he was not capable of being a father, that her son would be much better off without him in his life? He supposed he could explain the truth about his legacy, the barren emotional landscape of his own childhood. But he had humiliated himself enough for one day already with the confidences he'd been forced to share. And he suspected even if he told her the truth about his upbringing and how unsuitable it made him for the role she wished him to consider, it wouldn't be enough. Because Carmel O'Riordan appeared to be as stubborn as her brother's right hook.

Not only that, but he had no desire to unearth memories he had buried a lifetime ago.

He blew out a breath, struggling to calm the wayward emotions churning in his gut and find a tangible solution to the impasse. His gaze focussed on the rhythm of the surf, as it crashed against the rocks below, then retreated down the beach of the small cove.

The spring sunshine glinted off the water, the vibrant green Ireland was famous for carpeting the cliffs and spreading over the castle's gardens. A few guests from the wedding were milling about near the entrance to the chapel. His gaze snagged on a small child with a couple, the woman noticeably pregnant. His heart stilled, his exhaustion and frustration momentarily forgotten as he watched the child, so active and carefree, dashing backwards and forwards as the man—a strapping redhead who looked uncomfortable in his suit—chased after him while the woman directed the action and appeared to be finding it extremely amusing. He squinted, the gritty fatigue making his eyes smart.

Wait a minute, is that boy...?

He turned swiftly away from the window, the pressure on his chest increasing, to find Carmel watching him with a disturbing intensity—almost as if she could see into his thoughts.

Good luck with that, he thought, careful to keep the turmoil of emotions off his face.

And suddenly, he knew the only solution to this impasse was to show her exactly what kind of emotional connections he was and was not capable of.

With her hip cocked and her arms crossed, her stance accentuated her lithe figure. The sun shone off her haphazard hairdo and gave her fair skin a lustrous glow. But this time, instead of steeling himself against the inevitable spike to his libido, he welcomed it.

He could do sex. He couldn't do commitment. He never had—which was why that energetic, carefree little boy was much better off without a man like him in his life. That was the truth of the matter, and the only truth Carmel O'Riordan needed to understand.

She was clearly a smart and forthright woman. It was one of the things he'd found so compelling about her that night, her ability to speak her mind with wit and courage and refreshingly little thought to the consequences. It had amused him and intrigued him and aroused him immensely, perhaps because he had always been forced to guard his own emotions so carefully.

But—although she'd had to grow up far too fast in the years since—she still seemed to be hopelessly naïve about men.

'I think the problem we have, Carmel, is that you don't know me,' he ventured. 'We've had one…' *Exciting? Mind-blowing? Cataclysmic?* He cleared his throat, to give himself time to search for the appropriate adjective. 'Diverting night together. And not much else. Perhaps you should spend some time with me? Then you'd realise I'm not a man you would want in your life long-term.' He stepped closer and touched his thumb to her cheek. She sucked in a breath, her eyes darkening, as he hooked one errant tendril behind her ear, then forced himself to drop his hand. The contact had been electrifying, just as he had expected it would be, making his point for him admirably. 'Nor am I father material.'

It was a dare, pure and simple. A dare he doubted she would accept.

The spark was still there, waiting to explode all over again. And given what that had led to last time, how could she afford to risk reigniting the flame?

She gave her head a slight shake, as if she had gone into a trance and was waking up again. He watched the emotions flit across her face—surprise, confusion, yearning…and panic as the penny dropped.

Bingo.

However naïve she was, or inexperienced she had been then, she knew full well they would both be playing with fire if she accepted his offer.

He pressed his hands back into his pockets, to resist the powerful urge to touch her again. And ignored the strange ambivalence at the realisation she would not accept his impulsive offer.

But then her true-blue eyes sparkled with the same recklessness he had once admired so much and her lips pursed in a thin line of determination.

'I accept, I think that's a grand idea,' she said. 'Spending time with you in your home would be the best way to assess your lifestyle as well as your suitability to be a daddy to Mac. I can come with you today if you'd like as Mac is already supposed to be spending this week with my sister, Immy, and her husband, Donal, while I finish a commission. Would it be okay if I brought my paints with me, so I can work?'

'You want to come with me? Today?' he said, astonished not just by her reckless decision, but also by the brutal wave of arousal. 'And stay for a week?'

'Yes. Where do you live?' she asked.

'New York,' he croaked, the blood diving south as he envisioned her in his condo in Tribeca. It was a big space, but hardly big enough to house them both without him being far too aware of her presence. He'd never invited any woman into his home for any length of time. Sleepovers at his apartment and the occasional weekender at his estate in the Hamptons were fine, but nothing more than that. When it came to women, he preferred to hold all the cards. But it already felt as if he had somehow dropped the ace.

'Really? I've never been to New York before. I've heard it's glorious.' She pushed her hair back from her face, the flush lighting her cheeks and the nervous gesture suggesting she wasn't as composed as she was making out—which was some consolation, but not much.

'I'll need a bit of time to pack and square things with Mac and my family.' She huffed out a breath. 'Especially Conall. When do you want to leave?'

He stared at her. She was actually serious. She intended to come and spend a week with him in New York.

A part of him knew at this point he should call her bluff. Rescind the offer, because he had no real desire to open up his life or his motivations to her scrutiny, but something stopped him. Perhaps it was the emotional fatigue finally getting to him after the seven-hour overnight journey to Ireland on a mission to protect the sister he'd barely spoken to in years. Perhaps it was the shock of seeing the woman who had haunted his dreams for so long again and discovering he was a father, against all the odds. Or maybe it was the residual heat still humming in his groin. But whatever it was, he couldn't seem to think anything but... *To hell with it*. Perhaps this really was the best way to persuade her he could never be a father to her son.

'I'd like to leave as soon as possible,' he said. If she was coming, she needed to know her visit would be on his terms, not hers. 'Can you be ready in an hour?'

'Give me two,' she said. 'I'd like you to meet Mac before we leave. We won't tell him who you are. Not yet. But it should keep us both focussed on why we're doing this.'

Ya think?

Exactly how naïve was she? Did she really

think him coming face to face with the boy
would be enough to kill this incessant heat?

'Sure,' he said, deciding meeting the boy
would be a good first step in persuading her he
knew absolutely nothing about children.

But as she left the room, his gaze snagged on
the subtle sway of her hips in the figure-hugging
bridesmaid's gown and the heat swelled again.

*Wonderful. The next week is going to be noth-
ing short of torture and you have only yourself
to blame.*

CHAPTER FOUR

'YOU'RE NOT GOING. I won't allow it. Have you lost your mind?'

Mel glared at her older brother, feeling her hackles rising fast enough to break the land-speed record. If there was one thing Conall had always been an expert at, it was making her mad.

'Er…hello, Con? I'm a grown woman, and this is not your decision,' she replied, channelling a certainty about the trip she didn't remotely feel.

With Con's tie and tuxedo jacket gone and his skin slightly flushed from one too many toasts during the wedding feast, he should have looked more relaxed, but the muscle twitching in his jaw was suggesting the opposite. He'd stayed away from her meeting with Ross, given her the privacy she'd asked for. And she had to give him credit for that—or rather give Katie credit for it. Because she suspected Con's new wife had managed to drum some sense into him, and also provided a gorgeous distraction. Her new sister-in-law stood beside Con now, looking completely stunning in her wedding dress—and apparently not remotely concerned at the two of them for ruining even more of her special day with their family drama.

'You're also a mother,' her brother added, his tone darkening. 'Have you thought of that, now?' he finished, slicing right to the heart of her insecurities. Another of her brother's specialities.

She'd never left Mac for more than a night before. But they'd been building up to his week staying with Imelda and her husband Donal for weeks now—because her work had exploded in the last few months, and she had an important commission to finish. Conall was right, it would be impossibly hard to leave Mac for a week, but she also knew full well the separation was likely to be much harder for her than her son.

Mac had always been a supremely confident and outgoing child. And she had her family to thank for that. They'd always been close-knit as siblings, having been orphaned when she and her sister were only eight and six and Con a young man of eighteen. They'd had a fair few rocky moments and some major blow ups in the years after her mother's death—with Conall as their guardian giving up what was left of his youth to become a mother and father to both her and

Immy. But when she'd come home from London pregnant and alone that summer—and broken by Ross De Courtney's rejection—Imelda and Con hadn't hesitated to step up and help her heal. Sure, they'd judged, especially Con, but they'd also offered their unconditional support. Because of them, and now Donal and Katie too, Mac understood he was part of a much bigger unit than just the two of them. Surely that explained why he was such a robust, well-adjusted little guy, despite being the son of a nineteen-year-old single mum who'd had no clue what to do when he'd first been put into her tired arms after six excruciating hours of labour.

She knew how lucky she was to have such a solid, unwavering support network—and she was grateful for it. But she also knew that if there was a chance Mac could have a father of his own, she wasn't wrong to explore that possibility. She'd already spoken to Imelda in detail about her plans to contact Mac every day over a video app—and if Imelda reported any signs of distress, she would come straight back to Ireland on the next flight.

But having Con look at her with that accusatory glare in his eye had her confidence wavering.

'Of course, I know that, Con,' she said with a firmness she didn't feel. 'But I'm doing this for Mac to see if there's a chance Ross can be a father to him,' she said, but she could hear the defensiveness. And the questions she hadn't wanted to address—ever since Ross had touched her and the yearning had exploded inside her— whispered across her consciousness.

What if spending time with Ross De Courtney made that hunger worse? A hunger she'd had no practice in controlling because, not only had she never felt such a thing for another man, she'd never had sexual relations with any other man either.

'Ah, so going off to spend a week with your ex-lover is in your son's best interests now, is it?' Conall said, scepticism dripping from every word. 'That sounds mighty convenient to me.'

She stared at him, wanting to be furious with his implication, but not quite able to be... Because, what if he was right? And that shocking blast of heat and yearning *was* the real reason she'd decided to accept Ross's invitation? An invitation that she was sure had been born of frustration rather than intent.

She'd hate herself if she was subconsciously harbouring some secret notion to get Ross De Courtney into her life, as well as her son's. It would make her sad and pathetic and weak. And totally misguided. Because if the man wasn't father material, he certainly wasn't cut out for any other form of committed relationship. But worst of all, it would remind her of the little girl she'd once been, wanting her mother to love her, even though she could not.

'Conall, stop,' Katie said gently but firmly, interrupting the panicked questions multiplying in Carmel's head. 'Carmel has every right to make decisions for herself and Mac without having to deal with the third degree from you.'

'For the love of…' Con swore under his breath. Katie barely blinked. 'Katherine, why are you siding with her now?' Conall asked, sounding aggrieved. 'Maybe your brother isn't the total gobshite I thought he was,' he added, because Carmel had shared with them Ross's reasons for thinking he couldn't possibly be Mac's father— the news of his vasectomy at the age of only twenty-one having stunned them both into silence. 'But he's still not a man I'd trust with my sister for a week in a foreign country,' he added, speaking to his wife as if Carmel weren't standing right there, before levelling her with a look that teetered uncomfortably between concern and condescension. 'The man's a player, Mel, and a billionaire one at that, who's never had a serious relationship with anyone in his life, not even with his own sister,' he added. 'On that evidence, I'm not convinced he could ever be a halfway decent parent to Mac…'

'Fair point,' she interrupted him. 'But I want a chance to find out for my—'

'I get that,' Con said, cutting off her explanation. 'You want Mac to have his daddy in his life if at all possible. And maybe De Courtney will surprise us on that score. But is jetting off to New York with him so you guys can spend a cosy week...' he lifted his fingers to do sarcastic air quotes '..."Getting to know each other" really the way to go? What does that even entail? Are you going to be sharing a bed with him now?'

'Conall!' Katie gasped.

At exactly the same moment Carmel shouted, 'That's none of your business, Con.'

Of all the pig-headed, intrusive... How dared he?

Outrage flooded through her system, pushing away her doubts—and the echoes of that sad little girl—to remind her of the woman she had become. 'But just so you know, the answer is no.'

She was being ridiculous, she decided. So *what* if she was still attracted to Ross De Courtney? Surely it was to be expected. After all, he was the only man she'd ever had sex with. And he was... She took a steadying breath, aware of the liquid weight that had been there ever since he'd walked back into her life two hours ago now. Well, the man was a total ride and he always had been.

But the important thing here wasn't Ross De Courtney's hotness, it was the fact that she wasn't that starstruck, needy, reckless nineteen-year-old any more—nor was she the little girl without a mother's love. She was a mother herself now, with her own thriving online business doing pet portraits—and she'd had her heart broken once before by Ross. In short, she was all grown up now. She'd worked hard to build a life for her and her son, and there was no way she'd throw it all away for some cheap thrills. However tempting.

'Fine, I'm sorry.' The muscle in Conall's jaw softened and he had the decency to look contrite. 'I overstepped with that remark,' he murmured. 'It's just…' He drew close and gathered her into a hug. 'I'm your big brother. And I don't want to see you hurt by him again.'

She softened against him, the comforting scent of his cologne and the peaty smell of good Irish single malt whiskey gathering in her throat. Banding her arms around his waist, she hugged him back, aware of how far they'd come since that miserable Christmas morning when Con had found their mother dead…

She'd pushed her brother away so many times in the years after that dreadful event, especially as a teenager, when she'd acted out at every opportunity—to test his commitment, she realised now. They'd had some epic shouting matches as a result, but he'd always stuck regardless. Because Con wasn't just pig-headed and arrogant with a fiery temper that matched her own, he was also loyal to a fault and more resilient and hard-wearing than the limestone of the cliffs outside.

Her eyes stung as she drew back to gaze up at his familiar face. 'You've been much more than just a big brother to me, Con. So much more. And I appreciate it. But you've got to trust me on this. I know what I'm doing, okay?'

He drew in a careful breath and let it out slowly, clearly waging a battle with himself not to say any more on the subject. But at last he nodded. 'Okay, Smelly,' he said, using the nickname he'd first coined when—according to family legend—he'd had to change one of her nappies.

She laughed, because he knew how much she'd always hated that fecking nickname. Trust Con to get the final word.

But then he cupped her shoulders and gave her a paternal kiss on the forehead. 'I do trust you,' he murmured. 'And anyhow, if he hurts you again, I'll murder him. So there's that,' he added, only half joking, she suspected.

She forced her lips to lift in what she hoped was a confident smile as her eyes misted.

Now all she needed to do was learn how to trust herself with Ross De Courtney.

Grand! No pressure, then.

CHAPTER FIVE

ROSS STOOD ON the grass near the Kildaragh heliport, next to the company Puma he'd piloted from the airport in Knock to get to Conall O'Riordan's estate without delay what felt like several lifetimes ago, and braced as the O'Riordans headed towards him, en masse.

Carmel had changed out of the silky bridesmaid's dress into a pair of skinny jeans and a sweater, which did nothing to hide the lush contours of her lean body.

He stiffened against the inevitable surge of lust and shifted his gaze to the child—whose hand was firmly clasped in hers. The boy was literally bouncing along beside her, apparently carrying on a never-ending conversation that was making his mother smile.

The pregnant lady and the man he had spotted earlier in the gardens—who Ross had been informed by Katie were the other O'Riordan sibling, Imelda, and her husband, Donal—followed behind them. Conall O'Riordan, Ross's sister, and two footmen carrying a suitcase and assorted other luggage, brought up the rear.

He nodded to Katie as the party approached. He'd spoken to his sister ten minutes ago—a stilted, uncomfortable conversation, in which he'd apologised for disturbing her wedding and she'd apologised for not telling him sooner about his son's existence.

His sister sent him a tentative smile back now, but as Carmel approached him with the boy Katie held back with her husband and in-laws, making it clear they were a united front. United behind Carmel, and Ross was the outsider.

His ribs squeezed at the stark statement of his sister's defection. Even though he knew it was his own fault. He'd never been much of a brother to her, to be fair. He should have repaired the rift between them years ago. But thoughts of his sister disappeared, the pang in his chest sharpening, as Carmel reached him with the child.

'Hi, Ross. This is Cormac,' she said. She drew in a ragged breath. 'My son,' she added, her voice breaking slightly. 'He wanted to say hello to you before we left.'

'Hiya,' the little boy piped up, then waved. The sunny smile seemed to consume his whole face, his head tipped way back so he could see Ross properly.

Ross blinked, momentarily tongue-tied, as it occurred to him he had no idea how to even greet the boy.

Going with instinct, because the boy's neck position looked uncomfortable, he sank onto one knee, to bring his gaze level with the child's. 'Hello,' he said, then had to clear his throat when the word came out on a low growl.

But the boy's smile didn't falter as he raised one chubby finger to point past Ross's shoulder to the helicopter. 'Does the 'copter belong to yous?' he asked, the Irish accent only making him more beguiling.

Ross glanced behind him to buy himself some time and consider how to respond, surprised by the realisation that, even though this would most likely be the only time he would ever talk to his son, he wanted to leave a good impression... Or at least not a bad one. 'Yes, it belongs to my company,' he said, deciding to stick with the facts.

'It's bigger than my uncle Con's 'copter,' the little boy shot back.

Ross's lips quirked. 'Is it, now?' he replied, stupidly pleased with the comment.

At least I've managed to best Conall O'Riordan with the size of my helicopter.

The little boy nodded, then tipped his head to one side. 'Does it hurt?' he asked, his fingertip brushing across the swollen area on Ross's jaw.

Ross's throat thickened, the soft, fleeting touch significant in a way he did not understand. 'A bit.'

'It looks hurty,' the boy said. 'Mammy says it's naughty to hit people. Why did Uncle Con hit you?'

'Um, well…' He paused, completely lost for words. The tips of his ears burned as a wave of shame washed through him at the thought of how he and O'Riordan had behaved in front of this impressionable child. What an arse he'd been to take a swing at the man. 'Possibly he hit me because I tried to hit him first,' he offered, knowing the explanation was inadequate at best. 'And missed.'

'Cormac, remember Uncle Con told you it was a mistake and he's sorry.' Carmel knelt next to the boy. 'And I'm sure Ross is sorry too,' she added, sending him a pointed look.

Ross remembered how she'd mentioned she always addressed her son by his full name when he was being disciplined. But the child seemed unafraid at the firm tone she used, his expression merely curious as he wrapped an arm around his mother's neck and leaned into her body.

'I am sorry,' Ross said, because her stern look seemed to require that he answer.

'Yes, Mammy, but…' the little boy began,

turning to his mother and tugging on her hair. 'Still it *was* naughty now...'

'Mr De Courtney, we'll need to leave soon if we're going to make our departure time from Knock,' his co-pilot interrupted them.

'Okay, Brian, thanks.' Ross rose back to his feet. 'If you wish to say your goodbyes, I'll wait in the cockpit,' he said to Carmel, suddenly eager to get away from the emotion pushing against his chest—and the child who could never be a part of his life.

'Okay, I'll only be a minute,' Carmel said, the sheen of emotion in her eyes only making the pressure on his ribcage worse.

He dismissed it. What good did it do? Being intrigued by the boy? Moved, even? When he wasn't capable of forming a relationship with him?

'Goodbye, Cormac,' he murmured to the child, ignoring the fierce pang stabbing under his breastbone.

'Goodbye, Mr Ross,' the boy replied, with remarkable gravity for a child of such tender years. But as Carmel took her son's hand, to direct him back towards her family and say her goodbyes, the little boy swung round and shouted. 'Next time yous come we can play tag. Like I do with Uncle Donal.'

'Of course,' he said, oddly torn at the thought

he'd just made a promise he would be unable to keep... Because there would never be a next time.

'I think, in the circumstances, it would be best if we call a halt to this trip. I can have the helicopter take you back to Kildaragh.'

Carmel swung round to find Ross standing behind her in the private jet they'd just boarded at Knock airport. He looked tall and indomitable, and tired, she thought as she studied him. She waited for her heartbeat to stop fluttering—the way it had been for the last thirty minutes, ever since she had watched him speak to their son for the first time. She needed to get that reaction under control before they got to New York.

'Why would it be best?' she asked.

They'd travelled in silence after she'd bid goodbye to Mac and her family, the noise of the propellors too loud to talk as Ross had piloted the helicopter down the coast to Knock airport. She'd been grateful for the chance to collect her thoughts, still reeling from the double whammy of seeing Ross talk to Mac—and saying goodbye to her baby boy for seven whole nights.

She knew something about luxury travel—after all, her brother was a billionaire—but even so she'd been impressed by how quickly they'd been ushered aboard De Courtney's private jet, which had been waiting on the tarmac when they arrived. But she'd sensed Ross's growing reluctance as soon as they'd boarded the plane, the tension between them only increasing. The smell of new leather filled her senses now as she waited for Ross to reply.

His brow furrowed. 'Surely it's blatantly obvious after my brief conversation with the boy—this trip is pointless?'

'I disagree,' she said, surprised that had been his take away from the encounter.

Certainly, he'd been awkward and ill at ease meeting his son. That was to be expected, as she would hazard a guess he had very little experience of children. But she had also noticed how moved he'd been, even if he didn't want to admit it. And how careful.

'Mac likes you already,' she said, simply.

His frown deepened. 'Then he's not a very good judge of character.'

'On the contrary,' she said, 'he's actually pretty astute for a three-year-old.'

He shoved his hands into the pockets. 'So you still wish to accompany me?' he asked again.

'Yes, I do. If the offer is still open,' she said, suddenly knowing the conversation they were having wasn't just about their son. Because the air felt charged. On one level, that scared her. But on another, after seeing him make an effort to talk to his son openly and honestly, it didn't.

Perhaps he was right. Perhaps this trip was

a lost cause. After all, a week was hardly long enough to get to know anyone. Especially someone who seemed so guarded. But she was still convinced she had to try… And she was also coming to realise that there was more at stake here than just her son's welfare.

Didn't she deserve to finally know what had made her act so rashly all those years ago? She'd thrown herself at this man that night, revelled in the connection they'd shared, and a part of her had always blamed herself for that. Maybe if she got to the bottom of why he had captivated her so, she might be able to forgive that impulsive teenager for her mistakes. And finally let go of the little girl she'd been too, who had looked for love in places where it would never exist.

She waited for him to reply, her breath backing up in her lungs at the thought she might have pushed too hard. It was one of her favourite flaws, after all. And knowing she would be gutted if he backed out now and told her the trip was off.

The moment seemed to last for ever, the awareness beginning to ripple and burn over her skin as he studied her.

His eyes darkened and narrowed. Could he see how he affected her? Why did that only make the kinetic energy more volatile?

'The offer is still open,' he said, at last, and her breath released, making her feel light-headed. But then he stepped closer and touched his thumb to her cheek. He slid it down, making the heat race south, then cupped her chin and raised her face. 'But I should warn you, Carmel. I still want you,' he said, his voice rough with arousal. 'And that could complicate things considerably.'

Her lips opened, her breath guttering out, the anticipation almost as painful as the need as her gaze locked on his and what she saw in it both terrified and excited her. It was the same way he had looked at her all those years ago—focussed, intense—as if she were the only woman in the whole universe and he the only man.

She licked arid lips, and the heat in his gaze flared.

'Do you understand?' he demanded.

She nodded. 'Yes, I feel it too,' she said, not ashamed to admit it. Why should she be? She wasn't a girl any more. 'It doesn't mean we need act on it.'

He gave a strained laugh—then dropped his hand. 'Perhaps.'

'Mr De Courtney, the plane is ready to depart in ten minutes if you and Ms O'Riordan would like to strap yourselves in,' the flight attendant said, having entered the compartment unnoticed by either of them.

Ross's gaze lifted from her face. 'Thank you, Graham. I'm going to crash in the back bedroom. Make sure Ms O'Riordan has everything she needs for the duration of the flight.'

The attendant nodded. 'Of course, sir.'

Without another word to her, Ross headed towards the back of the plane.

She gaped. Had she just been dismissed?

The attendant approached her. 'Would you like to strap yourself in here and then I can show you to the guest bedroom when we reach altitude?'

'Sure, but just a minute…' she said, then shot after her host.

She opened the door she had seen Ross go into moments before. And stopped dead on the threshold.

He turned sharply at her entry, holding his torn shirt in his hand.

Oh. My.

She devoured the sight of his naked chest, her gaze riveted to the masculine display as the heat blazed up from her core and exploded in her cheeks.

The bulge of his biceps, the ridged six-pack defined by the sprinkle of hair that arrowed down beneath the waistband of his trousers, the flex of his shoulder muscles—were all quite simply magnificent.

'Was there something you wanted?' he prompted.

'I… Yes.' She dragged her gaze to his face,

the wry twist of his lips not helping with her breathing difficulties, or her burning face. She sucked in a lung full of air and forced herself to ask the question that had been bothering her for nearly an hour. 'I just wanted to ask you, what made you kneel when you met him? Mac, that is?' she managed, realising the sight of his chest had almost made her forget her own son's name.

He threw away his shirt, clearly unbothered by his nakedness. 'Why do you want to know that?'

'It's just… You say you don't know anything about children. But it was thoughtful and intuitive to talk to him eye to eye like that. I was impressed. And so was Mac.'

'Hmm,' he said, clearly not particularly pleased by the observation. 'And you think this makes me a natural with children, do you?' he said, the bitter cynicism in the tone making it clear he disagreed.

'I just wondered why you did it,' she said, letting her own impatience show. The jury was still out on his potential as a father, and she only had a week to decide if she wanted to let him get to know her son. But she didn't see how they could make any progress on that unless he was willing to answer a simple question. 'That's all.'

'I'm afraid the answer is rather basic and not quite as intuitive as you believe,' he said, still prevaricating.

'Okay?' she prompted.

He sighed. 'My father was a tall man. His height used to intimidate me at that age. I didn't wish to terrify the boy, the way my father terrified me. Satisfied?'

'Yes,' she said, the wave of sympathy almost as strong as the spurt of hope.

Perhaps this didn't have to be a lost cause at all.

He began to unbuckle his belt, his gaze darkening. 'Now I suggest you leave, unless you want to join me in this bed for the duration of the flight.'

'Right.' She scrambled out of the room, slamming the door behind her.

It was only once she had snapped her seat belt into place that it occurred to her she was more excited by his threat than intimidated by it.

Uh-oh.

CHAPTER SIX

WHAT AM I even doing here?

Carmel stood at the floor-to-ceiling window of Ross De Courtney's luxury condo and stared through the glass panes of the former garment factory at the street life below as Tribeca woke up for another day.

The guest room she'd been given was a work of art—all dramatic bare brick walls and vaulted arches, steel columns, polished walnut wood flooring and minimalist furniture, which included a bed big enough for about six people, and an en suite bathroom designed in stone and glass brick. The room even had its own roof terrace, beautifully appointed with trailing vines, wrought-iron furniture and bespoke lighting to create an intimate and yet generous outdoor space.

The views were spectacular, too. At seven stories up she could see the tourist boats on the Hudson River a block away and the New Jersey waterfront beyond, to her left was the dramatic spear of the One World Trade Center building, and below her was the bustle and energy of everyday New Yorkers—dressed in their trademark uniform of business attire and trainers—flowing out of and into the subway station on the corner or dodging the bike couriers and honking traffic to get to work, most of them sporting go-cups of barista coffee.

She knew something about luxury living from the glimpses she'd had of her brother's lifestyle. But Ross De Courtney's loft space, situated in the heart of one of Manhattan's coolest neighbourhoods, was something else—everything she had thought high-end New York living would be and more. But the edgy energy and purpose of all the people below hustling to get somewhere—and the stark modernity of the exclusive space she was staying in—only made her feel more out of place. And alone.

She'd been here for over twenty-four hours already, after arriving on the flight across the Atlantic. And while she'd spent a productive day yesterday—in between several power naps—exploring Ross's enormous loft apartment, the local area, and setting up a workstation with the art supplies she'd brought with her in the apartment's atrium, she'd barely seen anything of the man she'd come here to get to know.

She sighed, and took a sip of the coffee she'd spent twenty minutes figuring out how to brew on his state-of-the-art espresso machine after waking up before dawn.

Thank you, epic jet lag!

He'd dropped her off late at night after their flight and a limo ride from the airport, during which he'd spent the whole time on his phone. Once they'd arrived at the apartment, he'd told her to make herself at home, given her a set of keys and a contact number for his executive assistant, and then headed straight into his offices because he apparently had 'important business'.

And she hadn't seen him since.

She didn't even know if he was in residence this morning. She'd tried to stay up the previous evening, to catch him when he returned from work, but had eventually crashed out at around eight p.m., New York time. And slept like the dead until four this morning. She hadn't heard him come in the night before, and there had been no sign he'd even been in the kitchen last night during her adventures with the espresso machine this morning.

Is he avoiding me?

She took another gulp of the coffee, the pulse of confusion and loneliness only exacerbated by the memory of her truncated conversation over her video messaging app with her baby boy five minutes before.

'Mammy, I can't talk to yous. Uncle Donal is taking me to see the horses.'

'Okay, fella, shall I call you tomorrow?'
'Yes, bye.'

And then he'd been gone, and Imelda had appeared, flushed and smiling. 'Thanks so much for letting us have him for the week, Mel,' she'd said as she cradled her bump. 'We need the practice for when this little one arrives and he's doing great so far. He went to bed without complaint last night.'

'Ah, that's grand, Immy,' she'd replied, stupidly tearful at the thought her little boy was doing so well. Even better than she had expected. And a whole lot better than her.

She missed him, so much.

Not seeing his face first thing when she woke up had been super weird. Especially now she was questioning why she'd flown all this way to get to know a man who didn't seem to want to know her. Or Mac.

'You must contact me if there's any problem at all,' she'd told her sister, almost hoping Imelda would give her the excuse she needed to abandon what already seemed to be a fool's quest. 'I can hop straight on a flight if need be.'

'Sure, of course, but Mac's grand at the moment, he hasn't mentioned missing you once,' Imelda had said, with typical bluntness. Then she had sent Carmel a cheeky grin. 'How's things going with Mac's uber-hot daddy?'

'I'm not here to notice how hot he is, Immy,'

she'd replied sternly, aware of the flush hitting her own cheeks—at the recollection of Ross without his shirt on in the close confines of the jet's bedroom. 'I'm here to get to know him a bit better and discuss Mac with him, and his place in his son's life. That's all.'

'Of course you are, and that's important for sure,' her sister had said, not making much of an effort to keep the mischievous twinkle out of her eyes—which was even visible from three thousand miles away. 'But sure there's no reason now not to notice what a ride he is at the same time.'

Oh, yes, there is, Immy. Oh, yes, there is.

She pressed her hand to her stomach, recalling the spike of heat and adrenaline at her sister's teasing before she'd ended the call, which was still buzzing uncomfortably in her abdomen now. Trust Imelda to make it worse.

The loud ring of the apartment's doorbell jerked her out of her thoughts. And had hot coffee spilling over her fingers. She cursed, then listened intently as she cleaned up the mess and tiptoed to the door of her bedroom to peek out.

If Ross answered the door, she'd at least know if he was here. Then she could waylay him before he left again. Perhaps they could have breakfast together? Although the thought of Ross De Courtney in any kind of domestic setting only unsettled her more.

The bell rang a second time and then she heard something else... Was that a dog barking?

Surprise rushed through her, which turned to visceral heat as the man himself appeared on the mezzanine level above and padded down the circular iron staircase from the apartment's up-stairs floor. In nothing but a pair of shorts and a T-shirt, with his hair sleep-roughened and his jaw covered in dark stubble, it was obvious the doorbell had woken him.

The buzz in Carmel's abdomen turned to a hum as he scrubbed his hands down his face before walking past her hiding place to the apartment's front door.

Her gaze fixed on his back as he began the process of unlocking the several different latches on the huge iron door and the dog's barks became frenzied.

The worn T-shirt stretched over defined muscles, accentuating the impressive breadth of his shoulders. Carmel's gaze followed the line of his spine to the tight muscles of his glutes, displayed to perfection in stretchy black boxers.

Then he opened the door and all hell broke loose.

Surprise turned to complete astonishment as a large, floppy dog bounded into the room, its toenails scratching on the expensive flooring, its barks turning to ecstatic yips.

'Hey, boy, you missed me?' Ross said, his

deep voice rough as the animal jumped to place its gigantic paws on his chest. What breed was that exactly?

A smaller person would surely have been bowled over by the dog's enthusiastic greeting, but Ross braced against the onslaught, obviously used to the frenzied hello, and managed to hold his ground as the huge hound lavished him with slobbering affection.

Ross De Courtney has a dog? Seriously?

She waited, expecting him to discipline the dog, but instead he rubbed its ears and a deep rusty laugh could be heard under the dog's barking.

'Relax, Rocky,' he said, eventually grabbing the dog's collar and managing to wrestle it back onto all fours. 'Now, sit, boy,' he said, with all the strident authority of a Fortune 500 Company CEO. The dog gave him a goofy grin and ignored him, its whole body wagging backwards and forwards with the force of its joy.

'Rocky, sit!' The incisive command was delivered by a small middle-aged woman dressed in dungarees and biker boots—her Afro hair expertly tied back in a multi-coloured scarf—who must have brought the dog and followed it into the apartment.

The dog instantly dropped its butt, although the goofy grin remained fixed on Ross as if he were the most wonderful person in the known universe.

'How the heck do you do that, Nina?' Ross murmured, sounding disgruntled as the woman produced a treat and patted the dog's head.

Carmel grinned, feeling almost as goofy as the dog, her astonishment at the animal's appearance turning into a warm glow.

Ross De Courtney has a dog who adores him.

'Practice,' the dog trainer said as she unloaded a bowl, a blanket and a lead from her backpack. After dropping them on the kitchen counter, she gave the dog a quick scratch behind the ears before heading back towards the door. 'You've gotta show him who's boss, Ross. Not just tell him.'

'Right,' Ross replied, still endearingly disgruntled. 'I thought I was.'

'Uh-huh.' The woman snorted, her knowing smile more than a little sceptical. 'Dogs are smart, they know when someone's just playing at being a badass.'

They had a brief conversation about plans for the coming week—Nina was obviously his regular dog walker and sitter and had been looking after Rocky while Ross was out of the country—before the woman left.

Carmel stood watching from behind the door to her room, aware she was eavesdropping again, but unable to stop herself. A bubble of hope swelled under her breastbone right next to the warm glow as she observed Ross interact with his devoted pet. Talking in a firm, steady voice, he calmed the animal down, rewarded him every time he did as he was told, and fed and watered him, before pouring himself a mug of coffee and tipping a large helping of psychedelic cereal into a bowl. The rapport between Ross and the animal—which Carmel eventually decided was some kind of haphazard cross between a wolfhound and a Labrador—was unmistakable once the dog stretched out its lumbering limbs over the expensive rug in the centre of the living area for a nap.

Questions bombarded her. How old was the dog? How long had it been his? Where had he got it? Because it looked like some kind of rescue dog. Definitely a mongrel crossbreed and not at all the sort of expensive pedigree status symbol she would expect a man in his position to own if he owned a pet at all. Especially a man who had insisted he didn't do emotional attachments.

The bubble of hope became painful.

Maybe it was the jet lag, or the emotional hit of her earlier conversation with Mac, or simply the weird disconnect of being so far away from home—and so far outside her comfort zone— with a man who still had the power to make her ache after all these years… But this discovery felt significant. And also strangely touching.

That Ross De Courtney not only had a softer side he hadn't told her about. But one he'd actively refused to acknowledge.

Ross gave a huge yawn, and raked his fingers through his hair, carving the thick chestnut mass into haphazard rows.

The swell of emotion sharpened into something much more immediate. And the hum in her abdomen returned, to go with the warm glow. She cleared her throat loudly, determined to ignore it.

Ross's head lifted, and his gaze locked on her.

The heat climbed into her cheeks and bottomed out in her stomach.

'You're up early,' he said, the curt, frustrated tone unmistakable. 'How long have you been standing there?'

The easy camaraderie he'd shown the dog had disappeared, along with his relaxed demeanour. He had morphed back into the brooding billionaire again—guarded and suspicious and watchful.

The only problem was, it was harder to pull off while he was seated on a bar stool in his shorts with a bowl of the sort of sugary cereal Mac would consider a major treat. She'd seen a glimpse of the man who existed behind the mask now and it had given her hope.

She walked into the room, brutally aware a second too late she hadn't changed out of her own sleep attire when his gaze skimmed over her bare legs—could he tell she wasn't wearing a bra? The visceral surge of heat soared.

But she forced herself to keep on walking. Not to back down, not to apologise, and most of all to keep the conversation where it needed to be.

'Long enough,' she said. 'So just answer me this, Ross. You have the capacity to love Rocky here.' The dog's ears pricked up at the sound of his name and he bounded towards her. She laughed at the animal's greeting, surprised but also pleased to see that up close he was an even uglier dog than she'd realised, one ear apparently chewed off, his snout scarred and his eyes two different colours—one murky brown, the other murky grey. 'But you don't have the capacity to love your own child? Is that the way of it?'

'It's hardly the same thing,' Ross managed, furious she had spied on him, but even more furious at the spike of arousal as his houseguest bent forward to give Rocky's stomach a generous rub and her breasts swayed under soft cotton. 'A dog is not a child,' he added, trying to keep his mind on the conversation, and his irritation. And not the surge of desire working its way south.

He'd stayed at work until late in the evening last night, catching up on emails and doing conference calls with some of De Courtney's Asian offices precisely so he could avoid this sort of scenario. He'd had plans to be out today as soon as Nina dropped off Rocky, but he'd overslept. And now here they were, both virtually naked with only a goofy dog to keep them sane. While he'd missed his pet, Rocky wasn't doing a damn thing to stop the heat swelling in his groin.

'I know, but surely the ability to care and nurture is not that different,' she said as he tried to keep track of the conversation and not the way her too short nightwear gave him a glimpse of her panties as she bent over—and made her bare, toned legs look about a mile long. 'All I'm saying is if you have the capacity to care for Rocky here, why wouldn't you have the capacity to care for Mac?' she said, scratching his dog's head vigorously and laughing when Rocky collapsed on the floor to display his stomach for a scratch—like the great big attention junkie he was.

Heck, Rocky, show a bit of restraint, why don't you?

'Hey, boy, you like that, don't you?' she said, still chuckling, the throaty sound playing havoc with his control. The dog's eyes became dazed with pleasure.

He knew how Rocky felt as he watched her

breasts under the loose T-shirt—which shouldn't have looked seductive, but somehow was more tantalising than the most expensive lingerie.

Is she even wearing a bra?

The dog's tongue flopped out of the side of its mouth as it panted its approval, in seventh heaven now from the vigorous stomach rub.

Terrific, now he was jealous of his own dog.

He remained perched on the stool, grateful for the breakfast bar, which was hiding the strength of his own reaction.

She finished rubbing Rocky's belly, patted the animal and then rose, to fix that inquisitive gaze back on him. The forthright consideration in her bright blue eyes only made him more uncomfortable and on edge. Almost as if she could see inside him, to something that wasn't there... Or rather, something that he certainly did not intend to acknowledge.

'You didn't answer my question,' she said as she walked towards the breakfast bar.

He kept his gaze on her face, so as not to increase the torture by dwelling on the way the T-shirt barely skimmed her bottom.

When exactly had he become a leg man, as well as a breast man, by the way?

She perched on the stool opposite, hiding her legs at last.

This was precisely why he hadn't wanted to have her in his condo. Intrusive questions were bad enough, but the feel of his control slipping was far worse.

She cleared her throat.

'What was the question again?' he asked, because he'd totally lost the thread of the conversation.

'If you can form an attachment to Rocky, why would you think you can't form one to Mac?' she repeated, the flush on her cheeks suggesting she knew exactly where his mind had wandered. Why did that only make the insistent heat worse?

He took a mouthful of his Lucky Charms and chewed slowly, to give himself time to get his mind out of his shorts and form a coherent and persuasive argument.

He swallowed. 'A child requires a great deal more attention than a dog,' he murmured. 'And Nina spends almost as much time with Rocky as I do. Because I happen to be a workaholic.'

It was the truth.

He didn't have much of a social life, and that was the way he liked it. When he'd first taken over the reins of De Courtney's after his father's death he had resented the time and trouble it had taken to drag the ailing company into the twenty-first century, but he'd soon discovered he found the work rewarding. And he was good at it. Especially undoing all the harm his father had done with his autocratic and regressive approach to recruitment and training, not to mention innovation. The fact the bastard would be turning in his grave at all the changes Ross had made to De Courtney's archaic management structures was another fringe benefit. He'd never enjoyed socialising that much and had only attended those events where he needed to be seen. He had no family except Katie and he'd hardly spoken to her in years, and he had very few friends in New York—just a couple of guys he shared the occasional beer or squash game with. It was one of the reasons he'd moved to the US—he preferred his solitude and as much anonymity as he could have at the head of an international logistics conglomerate. And that just left his sex life, which he had always been careful to keep ruthlessly separate from other parts of his life.

All of which surely meant he wasn't cut out to be a father. No matter how easily he had bonded with Rocky, after finding the pup beaten and crying in a dumpster behind the apartment two summers ago. And he'd made a spur-of-the-moment decision to keep him.

But that hardly made him good parent material, not even close.

'That's true,' Carmel said, and nodded. 'A child does need your full attention at least some of the time. And I've already figured out how dedicated you are to your job.'

Something hollow pulsed in his chest, right alongside the surge of desire that would not die.

'I also live in New York, which would mean any time I could give Mac would be limited,' he added, determined to press home the point—despite the hole forming in his chest.

Her pensive look faded, and her lips curved upward, the blue of her irises brightening to a rich sapphire. The hollow sensation turned to something raw and compelling.

'Do you know? That's the first time you've called Mac by his name,' she said, her voice fierce, and scarily rich with hope.

'Is it?' he said, staring back at her, absorbing the shock to his system as he struggled not to react to her smile.

Good grief, the woman was even more stunning when she smiled. That open and forthright expression of pure uninhibited joy was a lethal weapon… How could he have forgotten the devastating effect her spontaneous smile had had on him once before? The driving need to please her, to hear her laugh, something that had effectively derailed all his common sense four years ago.

He'd known it would be dangerous bringing her here. But the hit to his libido was nowhere near as concerning as the chasm opening up in his chest at the first sign of her approval.

'I think it's a very positive sign,' she said.

'I wouldn't read too much into it if I were

you,' he said, trying to counter her excitement. But even he could hear the defensiveness in his voice.

Where was that coming from?

He didn't need her approval, or anyone's. He didn't need validation, or permission for the way he had chosen to live his life—avoiding forming the kind of emotional attachments she was speaking about. That hollow ache meant nothing. He'd stopped needing that kind of validation as a boy, when he'd discovered at a very young age his father didn't love him—and never would. That he was simply a means to an end. He didn't consider it a weakness, he considered it a strength. Because as soon as he'd finally accepted the truth, he'd worked on becoming emotionally self-sufficient.

And, okay, maybe Rocky had sneaked under his guard. But he didn't have room for any more emotional commitments. Why couldn't she accept that?

He opened his mouth to say exactly that, but before he could say any of it she said, 'You haven't said whether you want to be a father or not. Just that you can't be one.'

'I had a vasectomy when I was twenty-one,' he said, but even he could hear the cop-out in his answer. 'I think that speaks for itself.'

'Does it?' she said, far too astute for her own good, looking at him again with that forthright expression that suggested she could see right into his soul… A soul he'd spent a lifetime protecting from exactly this kind of examination, a soul that suddenly felt transparent and exposed. 'Because I'd say your reasons for having that vasectomy are what's really important, and you haven't explained them to me.'

'I didn't want to be a father,' he said flatly, but the lie felt heavy on his tongue, because she was right. It had never been about whether or not he *wanted* to be a father. He'd never even asked himself that question. It had always been much more basic than that. It had always been about not wanting to get a woman pregnant.

She crossed her arms over her chest, looking momentarily stricken by his answer. But then her gaze softened again. 'But now you are one, how do you feel about Mac?'

'Responsible. And terrified,' he said, surprising himself by blurting out the truth.

'Terrified? Why?' she pushed. The bright sheen of hope and excitement in her gaze—as if she'd made some important breakthrough, as if she had found something he knew wasn't there—only disturbing him more.

'That I'll do to him what my father did to me,' he said. 'And his father did to him. There's a legacy in the De Courtney family that no child should have to be any part of,' he said, determined to shut down the conversation.

But instead of her backing down, instead of her realising he was a lost cause—that he couldn't offer their son what didn't exist—the glow in her eyes only softened more.

'What did he do to you, Ross, that you would be terrified now to have a child of your own?' she asked.

The probing question, the glow of sympathy made the pain in his gut tangle with the need. And the hollow ache twisted—turning to impotent fury.

What right did she have to ask him questions he didn't want to answer? To probe and to push, to open the raw wound of his childhood and make that pain real again?

'He did nothing to me that I didn't get over a long time ago,' he said, his voice a husky growl, wanting to believe it.

'I don't believe you,' she said, her voice coming from miles away, through the buzzing in his ears. But then she reached across the breakfast bar and covered his hand with hers. Her touch—warm, deliberate, provocative, unashamed—ignited the desire like a lightning strike, turning the fury to fire.

He flipped his hand over and grasped her wrist before she could withdraw her hand. She jolted. Her pulse thundered under his thumb but her eyes darkened, the need there as visceral and volatile as his own.

He might have been embarrassed at how much he wanted her. But he could see she wanted him too. Why the hell had he worked so hard to ignore it? Giving into it again had seemed fraught with problems, but, frankly, how could this be any more problematic than it already was?

She was the mother of his son. And nothing was going to change that now. However much he might want to turn back the clock and take this commitment away—it was too damn late. Had been too damn late four years ago, when he'd plunged inside her without using protection and created a life.

She was right about that much at least. All his efforts to deny this connection weren't going to make it not so. That little boy *did* deserve a father. However inadequate he might be for the job, he would have to stop hiding. But he'd be damned if he'd bare his soul while he was at it. And he'd be damned if he'd deny the other connection they shared any longer—which had been taunting and tormenting them both as soon as he'd spotted her at the wedding.

Keeping hold of her wrist, he got off the stool and walked round the breakfast bar, not even sure what he planned to do any more, but feeling his emotions slipping out of his grasp again.

He stood in front of her, and tugged her off her stool, the force of his passion throbbing painfully in his boxers.

'I've got a child now and there's no changing that,' he admitted, knowing he'd been a coward not to acknowledge that before now. 'And you're right, whatever my misgivings, he deserves at least as much of my attention as Rocky. But right now, I don't want to talk about that.' And he certainly had no intention of ever sharing with her why he had struggled to come to terms with that truth. His childhood was ancient history. Unearthing it now would only make this transition more difficult.

Oddly the concession didn't fill him with panic as it had before. The child was bright, sweet, unbearably cute. He could never be a full-time father to the boy, and he would need to learn on the job, but maybe she was right about that too. She had been forced to figure it out. And if he could love Rocky, maybe he could find room in his heart to do a much better job than his father. Surely at the very least he couldn't possibly do as much harm. And he owed it to the lad to try. And to stop running.

'Because all I can think about is having you again.' He let his gaze roam over her face, then lifted one hand to cradle one heavy breast. He felt the nipple pebble into a hard peak beneath his thumb.

Yup, no bra.

'And tasting every damn inch of you that I

didn't get to taste the first time,' he added, giving her fair warning.

He let her wrist go, giving her the choice.

But instead of pulling away, she looked him straight in the eye and then lifted up on tiptoes. She cupped his jaw, the trembling in her palm belied by the purpose in her eyes when she whispered against his lips, 'You don't scare me, Ross De Courtney.'

Then she clasped his face in her hands and pressed her lips to his.

He groaned as the fuse that had been lit long ago flared, sensation sparking through his body and turning the throbbing erection to iron. The need to claim her, to brand her as his, exploded along his nerve-endings, flooding his body like a river breaking its banks.

Grasping her waist, he lifted her into his arms, and carried her towards her guest bedroom, aware of the dog's playful barking through the pounding desperation.

His tongue thrust deep into the recesses of her mouth, gathering the sultry taste he remembered and taking control of the kiss.

He couldn't give her anything of real value. But he could give her this.

CHAPTER SEVEN

THE DOOR SLAMMED, cutting out the dog's bark. And Carmel found herself in her room alone with Ross, and the staggered sound of her breathing.

He let her go, her body sliding against the hard planes and angles of his, aware of the strident erection brushing her belly as she found her feet.

He kept his hand on her hip, holding her steady, her lips burning from the strength of his kiss.

This was madness. She knew that. But as she searched his face the pain she had glimpsed had been replaced with a fierce hunger. And the only way she could think of to free herself from that devastating feeling of connection was to feed it.

'Be sure,' he said, his voice as raw and desperate as she felt as his thumb brushed across her stinging lips with a tenderness, a patience she hadn't expected after that furious kiss.

'I am.' She nodded, struggling to speak around the lump jammed into her throat.

This was passion, desire, chemistry, part of a physical connection that had blindsided them both once before—it didn't need to mean more than that.

'Good,' he said, the word low with purpose.

But as his thumb trailed lower, slow, sure, steady, to circle the nipple poking against the cotton, her breath released in a rush and her knees weakened.

Holding her waist, he bent his head to fasten his lips on the aching tip and suckle hard through the fabric.

She thrust her fingers into his hair as moisture flooded between her trembling thighs.

Don't think. Just feel.

Every sense went on high alert as he lifted the wet T-shirt over her head, threw it away.

He swore softly, seeing all of her for the first time.

She folded her arms over her naked breasts, the rush of shyness stupid but unavoidable. Her body wasn't as tight and toned as it had once been. Before Mac. And he was the first man now, the *only* man to ever see her naked.

'Don't…' He groaned, the rough tone part demand, part plea. 'Don't hide yourself from me,' he said, but made no move to touch her.

He wanted this to be her choice, she could see

it in his eyes, the battle to hold himself back, to wait, as compelling as the need.

Don't think. Just feel. This is chemistry, basic and elemental, pure and simple.

She forced herself to unfold her arms and drop them to her sides. She arched her back, thrusting her breasts out, giving him the permission he sought. Refusing to be ashamed. Refusing to make this more than it was. Or ever could be.

This wasn't about the life they'd made together. She understood Mac had to be separate. Or she would be lost again, the way she had been once before. And she couldn't afford to be devastated again, by his rejection. She couldn't give him that power. Not now, not ever, when her little boy needed her whole. Always.

He scooped her up and placed her on the bed, then hooked his thumbs in the waistband of her panties and drew them down her legs.

She lay fully naked now, panting, as his gaze roamed over her, burning each place it touched. She could hide nothing from him, the bright morning light through the windows showing every flaw and imperfection the pregnancy had wrought on her once perfect skin.

His fingertip touched the silvery scars on her belly, and she squirmed, feeling more exposed than she ever had before, the desire retreating to be replaced with something raw and disturbing.

But when his head rose and his eyes met hers, emotion swirled in the blue-green depths.

'I want… I want to see you naked too,' she managed, trying to find that assertive, rebellious girl again. The girl she'd been that night, bold and determined before the emotion had derailed her.

He let out a laugh, low and strained. Then levered himself off the bed and stripped off his T-shirt. The masculine beauty of his chest looked even more magnificent, if that were possible, than it had in the jet. The ripple of muscle and sinew, the defined lines of his hip flexors and the sprinkle of hair circling flat nipples and trailing through the ridged board of his abs were as breathtaking as they were intimidating. But then he dragged his shorts down.

The strident erection sprang out. And her breath backed up in her lungs.

How did I ever manage to fit that inside me?

The panicked thought only seemed to intensify the liquid fire at her core.

He climbed on the bed, clasped her chin in firm fingers to raise her gaze. 'What's wrong?'

The heat flooded her cheeks. She blinked and licked bone-dry lips, clearing the rubble in her throat.

'No…nothing. Everything's grand.'

A bit too grand really, she thought wryly. Not

sure whether she wanted to laugh or cry at how gauche she felt.

He didn't know that he was the first—the only—man she had ever seen naked. That he was the only man who had ever been inside her. And she didn't want him to know, because that would only make her feel more vulnerable. And more like the frightened, overwhelmed girl she had been that night.

You're a woman now. Totally. Absolutely.

It didn't matter how little experience she still had of sex. She'd grown up in the years since that night in all the ways that mattered.

So stop blushing like a nun, you eejit.

'It's just... It's been a while now, since I've had sex,' she said, attempting to cover her gaffe. And feel less exposed to that penetrating, searching gaze. 'Being a mother is a full-time job.'

His lips crinkled in a rueful smile, only making her feel more gauche. The heat suffused her face like a forest fire.

'I can only imagine,' he murmured. 'Would you like me to slow down?'

She nodded, the emotion closing her throat and making her eyes burn, the comment reminding her of how he'd been that night. Passionate and provocative, yes, but also cautious and careful with her, until the need had overtaken them both.

Don't read too much into it. He's a pragmatic, methodical man. Why wouldn't he want to make it good for you?

'Tell me what you like,' he said.

She had no idea what she liked, but before she could come up with a creative lie he took the lead. His fingers skimmed down her body, circling her nipples.

Her back arched, the sensation shimmering again, the mortification forgotten as he bent to lick at one turgid tip, then the other.

'That…' she choked out, bowing back, lifting her breasts to him, the need surging again—sure and relentless and uncomplicated. 'I like that a lot.'

The gruff laugh rumbled out of his chest and through her body. But before she had a moment to wonder what was so amusing, he captured the pebbled peak and suckled.

She launched off the bed, the sensation arrowing down to her core, making her writhe and squirm as he held her steady and played with the too sensitive peaks, nipping and sucking and licking until her tortured groans became sobs.

At last he lifted his head, to blow across her swollen breasts, the contact too much and yet not enough. Then he grasped her hips, and began to lick a trail down her torso heading towards…

Oh, God… Oh, no. Will he taste me there?

His tongue caressed, circling her belly button, trailing lower still.

'Ah... Oh, God... Yes...' Her sobs became moans, the need so intense now she could barely breathe, no longer think, the twisting deep in her belly tightening like a vice.

Holding her hips, he angled her pelvis. 'Open for me, Carmel. I need to taste all of you.'

Her thighs loosened as if by his command, and his tongue found the heart of her at last, licking at the bundle of frayed nerves, sending shockwaves through her body.

She sobbed, panted. One long finger entered her, stretching the tight, tender flesh. Then two, while his lips remained fastened on the core of her pleasure, the vice tightening to the verge of pain.

She bucked against him, riding those delving fingers, impaling herself, ignoring the pinch to let the pleasure build.

She cried out as his mouth suckled, the waves building and building, the vice cinching into one unbearable torment. Fire tore through her and she cried out as the wave crashed over her at last, blasting through every fibre of her being, sending her high, only to drop her down to earth, shattered and shaking, sweating and worn through.

Her eyelids fluttered open, to find him above

her staring down, his eyes dark with a dangerous heat.

'You are so responsive,' he said. 'I adore watching you come.'

'I adore you making me come,' she said back, and was rewarded with a deep chuckle.

She hadn't meant to be funny, but somehow his amusement relaxed her. 'Do you have a condom?' she asked, desperate to feel him inside her now.

He nodded, the silent look reminding her of their aborted conversation about his vasectomy. The vasectomy that hadn't worked.

She'd touched a nerve there, she knew, asking him about his reasons for it. But when she'd reached for him a moment later, seeing the pain he'd been so determined to hide, it hadn't just been in sympathy. A part of her had wanted to ignite the heat, so she could forget that terrifying tug of connection.

He reached past her, delved in the bedside table, and found a foil packet. She watched, still shaky, still shattered, but oddly pleased to see how clumsy he was, how frantic he must be to have her too—to deny that connection as well—as he sheathed himself.

'I can't wait any longer,' he said.

She cupped his cheek, felt the stubble rasp against her palm, almost as raw as her emotions. 'Then don't,' she said, her voice sounding far away as the pounding in her ears became deafening.

Angling her hips, he notched himself at her entrance and pressed inside, the slick heat from her orgasm easing his way despite the tightness.

At last, he was lodged deep, so deep she could feel him everywhere.

'Okay?' he asked.

'Yes,' she murmured.

And then he began to move. Slow at first, but so large, so overwhelming.

His harsh grunts met her broken sobs as the fire built again, even faster and hotter than before. She clung to his broad shoulders and focussed desperately on the sound of their sweat-slicked bodies.

The waves gathered again, like a storm now, sensation driving sensation, every nerve-ending raw and real and unprotected, the pleasure battering her.

He shouted out as she felt him grow even bigger inside her, touching every single part of her, but as she broke into a thousand tiny pieces she was very much afraid this time he had shattered more than just her body, because she could still feel the deep, elemental pulse of connection in her heart.

CHAPTER EIGHT

THE AFTERGLOW DID nothing to stop the thunderous pulsing in Carmel's ears as Ross rolled away from her, then left the bed and walked into the en suite bathroom without a word.

The residual pulse of heat at the sight of his naked backside, the defined muscles flexing, did nothing for her galloping pulse. Or her shattered state of mind.

She dragged the bed's duvet up to cover herself.

Had she just done something phenomenally stupid, because, despite two staggering orgasms in the space of less than ten minutes, the emotions were still charging through her system—too raw, too real—and the yearning hadn't diminished in the slightest.

She could hear the water running in the en suite bathroom. Should she get up? Get dressed? With her body still humming from his caresses?

But worse than the physical impact on her body—which felt a little bruised now, after the intensity of their joining—was that devastating feeling of intimacy.

She had thought she wouldn't feel that again. Despite her lack of experience she wasn't a virgin any more—and she had new important priorities in her life now. But somehow, where she had hoped for mindless pleasure, what she'd got was far more dangerous. His care and attention had brought back so many memories from their first night. He had been focussed on her pleasure first and foremost then too, and it had made her yearn for so much more. For things she couldn't have and shouldn't need any more.

He appeared in the doorway, a towel slung around his hips.

The inevitable blush spread across her chest and suffused her cheeks.

Wow, awkward, much? Perhaps she should have considered this before she had chosen to jump into bed with him. Because the easy out—to lose herself in sex—now appeared to be anything but.

Then again, she was fairly sure she'd stopped thinking all together the moment he'd grasped her wrist, the purpose and passion in his gaze searing her skin.

'How are you?' he asked.

'Grand.' She blinked, mortified by the foolish sting of tears. She kept the duvet clasped to her chest and struggled to sit up, feeling far too vulnerable in her prone position on the bed.

It was a bit late for regrets, but one thing she couldn't bear was for him to think this interlude had meant more to her than it should. She'd made a conscious decision to sleep with him again, and it had been mind-blowing. She refused to regret that decision now. She could handle the fallout now the afterglow had faded—because she wasn't that emotional wreck of a girl any more. She couldn't be.

'I should probably get to work on my commission,' she said, hoping he would take the hint and leave—so she could get what had happened into some kind of perspective. It was just a physical connection. No more, no less. Why should it interfere with their shared priorities now as parents?

After all, before they'd jumped each other, Ross had made a major concession there. By finally admitting he needed—even wanted— to have a relationship with his son. That was huge. And so much more important than anything else. She still didn't really understand why he had struggled so to accept his place in Mac's life, or indeed why he had wanted a vasectomy so young… What exactly had his father done to him, to make him so convinced he should never be a parent himself? But surely it was best she didn't know the whys and wherefores.

Didn't probe into that lost look, which had resonated so strongly with the girl she'd been. She needed to protect herself now—couldn't let that needy girl back in. So all she really needed to know about that look was that he was prepared to move past it.

Instead of taking the hint, though, and leaving, Ross padded across the room's luxury carpeting and sat next to her on the bed. 'You're an artist, right?' he asked.

She swallowed, and nodded, surprised, not just by the intensity in his gaze, but the way it made her feel.

She'd told him about all her hopes and dreams that night—at the time, she'd been in her first term at art school with grand plans of becoming the next big thing on the Irish art scene—and he'd listened with the same intensity. In the years since—after she'd had to give up those dreams, or rather tailor them into something more useful—she'd dismissed his interest that night too. The thoughtful questions, the admiration in his gaze when she described her passions, had become just an effective means to get into her panties… And his technique had worked perfectly, because nothing could be more seductive to a girl who had lost her father at the age of six, and been at loggerheads with her brother ever since her mother's death two years later, than the wonder of uncritical male attention.

'So you found your dream?' he asked now, surprising her again. He remembered that too?

She gave a rough chuckle. 'Well, not precisely. I had to drop out of the Central Saint Martin's School of Art. And when I got back into the studio after Mac's birth, I had to make a living. But I like what I do.'

He frowned. 'What is it that you paint?'

'Portraiture. I specialise in dogs, actually. I love them and luckily for me so do my clientele. People are willing to pay quite a lot for a good likeness of their pet.'

His eyebrows rose but only a fraction. 'Do you and Mac have a dog?'

Her heartbeat clattered against her chest wall, her ribs squeezing. This was surely the first specific question he'd ever asked about their son. 'Mac adores dogs, but we can't afford one just yet. So he's happy hanging out with Imelda and Donal's two hounds when we need a doggie fix. I think he'd love to meet Rocky one day,' she ventured.

He nodded. 'I'm sure that can be arranged. Although I'd be concerned Rocky might knock him down. Rocky's quite big, Cormac is quite small and I'm still working on Rocky's manners.'

It was a thoughtful, considerate thing to say, so she couldn't resist asking.

'How did you end up picking him? He's a rescue dog, right?'

'Yeah. I didn't really pick him…he sort of picked me.'

'How so?' she asked, intrigued by the flags of colour on his cheeks. And trying not to let her gaze dip to his chest—which was having a far too predictable effect on her hormones again.

He sighed. And looked away.

'He was dumped in a trash can at the back of the apartment building as a puppy. Someone had beaten him quite severely. I heard his cries. Took him to the shelter. Two weeks later I rang to find out if he'd been successfully placed. And he hadn't. He's not the prettiest dog, as you probably noticed, but he's got a big heart.' He shrugged, as if his connection to his dog was a small thing, when she suspected it was massive. 'I'm not a sentimental man, but it seemed a shame to let him die after he'd fought so hard to stay alive.'

'I see,' she said, deeply touched by the story.

Ross De Courtney might believe he couldn't make emotional attachments, but Rocky proved otherwise.

'Is that why you called him Rocky? Because he's a fighter?'

'Yes,' he said, but then his intense gaze fixed back on her face. 'The marks, on your stomach, how did you get them?'

The blush reignited at the unexpected question—as she recalled how he'd trailed his fingers over the stretch marks while they were making love. Did he find them ugly?

'They're stretch marks. I got them when I was pregnant,' she said, bluntly, refusing to be embarrassed about the changes having his baby had made to her body—whatever he thought of them.

His Adam's apple bobbed as his throat contracted, and a muscle in his jaw hardened. He looked stricken, and she had no idea why.

'I was pretty huge when I got to the end of my pregnancy,' she offered, unable to read his reaction, suddenly needing to fill the silence—and take that stricken look out of his eyes. 'Mac was a big baby, nearly eleven pounds when he finally appeared. And, well, I slathered my belly in all sorts of concoctions, but it didn't…'

'Was it very painful?' he asked, interrupting the babbled stream of information with a direct look that could only be described as tortured.

'The stretch marks?' she asked.

'No, the birth.'

'Oh, yes, six hours of absolute agony,' she said with a small laugh, in a bid to lift the mood. But she realised her attempt at humour had backfired spectacularly when he paled.

She touched his arm, instinctively. 'Ross, what's wrong?'

'I'm sorry,' he said, the words brittle with self-loathing. A self-loathing she didn't understand.

'What for?' she asked.

'For putting you through that.' He stood, his whole body rigid with tension now.

'No need for an apology. I had a child I adore. The pain was totally worth it,' she said.

'That's not the point. I put your life at risk.'

'My...? *What?* No, you didn't.' She was so stumped now she didn't know what to say. He was totally overreacting, but his face had become an implacable mask again, rigid and unrelenting.

'I was only joking when I said it was total agony.' She paused, needing to be forthright now in the face of his... Well, she wasn't even sure what this was, or where it was coming from. But the emotion had been wiped off his face, to be replaced by the same intransigence she'd seen before. She didn't like it. 'Okay, to be fair it hurt, a lot, but I had every pain relief known to woman by the end of it. And my life was never in danger.'

He rewrapped the towel around his waist, making her far too aware of his nakedness and hers—the ripple of sensation tearing through what was left of her composure.

'I need to get to work,' he said, abruptly changing the subject. 'We can discuss the details later, but compensating you for your pain and suffering because of my carelessness is non-negotiable.'

'But…that's madness.' She sputtered, but then he grasped her chin, leaned down and pressed a kiss to her lips so possessive it cut off her thought processes entirely.

'We should probably also set some ground rules for the next week,' he added, letting her go. 'Sex-wise.'

The pragmatic comment had the blush firing into her cheeks.

How did he do that? Throw her completely for a loop without even trying? Because it was mortifying.

'What…what do you mean?' she said.

One dark eyebrow arched, and his gaze skimmed over her. She tightened her grip on the duvet—wondering for one panicked moment if he could see the hot weight lodged between her thighs that had started to pulse… *Again*.

'It's clear from what just happened that the exceptional chemistry between us is still very much there,' he said, the conversational, pragmatic tone belying the heat in his gaze and the brutal throbbing between her thighs. 'I figure we have two choices. We can either see that as a problem while you're here, in which case you should probably move into a hotel. Or we can enjoy it.'

'I…?' She stuttered, not sure what to say, or

how to react. Was it really that easy for him to completely separate the sex from the emotion? 'You'd be okay with that?'

Was that possible? To treat this urge as purely biological? She'd wanted to believe she could be as pragmatic as he was about the sex, but could she? How would she even know if she was capable of that, when she'd never had a relationship with any man before now? Never even had a fling. Except for her one night with him—which was basically a micro-fling.

'Of course,' he said, as if there was no doubt in his mind whatsoever.

Had he ever had a committed relationship? Because from the insouciance in his tone now, it seemed doubtful.

'But it would be your choice, obviously,' he said. 'Why don't you think about how you want to proceed, and we can discuss it tonight? I'll make sure I'm back at a reasonable hour…' His gaze dipped again, making her ribs squeeze uncomfortably and her nipples tighten. 'And we can have dinner together.'

'Umm… Okay,' she managed as he strolled out of the room.

As the door closed behind him, the soft thud echoed in her chest.

She flopped back on the bed, her whole body humming again from just the thought of 'discussing' their options 'sex-wise' tonight.

She had no idea what to think any more, or feel. But as she turned her head to gaze out of the paned-glass window, one thing she did know for sure…

Thinking about him, and her choices, was going to keep her brain tied in knots, and her body alive with sensation, for the hours until she saw him again.

CHAPTER NINE

A car will be arriving at seven p.m. to pick you up. I thought it would be best if we discuss our options over dinner on neutral ground. Any problems text me.

CARMEL PLACED HER brush down on the paint table, wiped her hands on the cloth she kept tucked into the waistband of her jeans and picked up her phone as if it were loaded with nitroglycerine.

She reread the message from Ross. Then read it again, struggling to absorb the shot of heat and panic. And something else entirely. Something that felt disturbingly like exhilaration. Which could not be good.

Then she checked the time.

It was already five. She only had two hours before she would see him again…

Where was he taking her? Because he hadn't bothered to specify.

For goodness' sake, she didn't even have a

single clue what to wear. Was he taking her to a restaurant? To talk about their sex life *in public*? Her cheeks burned... Was that the way of things in these situations? Did people do that in New York? Because they certainly didn't in rural Ireland.

She tapped out a reply as the panic—which she had spent six solid hours immersed in her art to try and control—tightened around her ribs again...

Where are we going?

But as she went to press 'send', her thumb hovered over the button.

She reread her reply, twice, and could hear her own lack of social savvy and confidence revealed in the words. Ross didn't know she'd been a virtual recluse since Mac was born, rebuilding her life from the ground up.

And she didn't want him to know. Would he blame himself for that too? And want to 'recompense' her for the fact she'd chosen to spend the last four years living a quiet life in County Galway learning how to be a mother?

She loved her quiet life. It worked for her, and Mac. And she'd found an outlet for her art that she loved too, she thought, glancing at the portrait she had lost herself in as she attempted to capture the winsome intelligence of a two-year-old cockapoo called Orwell.

She hadn't missed the social whirl she'd only glimpsed in passing in the few weeks she'd been in London at art school, and the night she'd first met Ross, once she'd returned home pregnant…

But somehow having him know how unsophisticated, and unsure she was about going for dinner in a fancy restaurant in New York—where everyone seemed to ooze confidence and style from every pore—would just add to her feelings of inadequacy where he was concerned. And make her feel as if she was at even more of a disadvantage when it came to discussing Mac's future relationship with his daddy… And what they were going to do 'sex-wise' over the coming week.

So don't ask him where you're going tonight, you eejit.

After all, talking about Mac would not be hard. There was so much she wanted to tell him about his son. And he seemed to have turned an important corner there this morning. When it came to the sex, all he was proposing was some fun while they got to know each other better and discussed their child's future. If they decided to go for it over the next week, to indulge themselves while she was here, it would be nothing more than a chance to blow off steam, to scratch an itch that had been there for four years—a quick fling with an end date already stamped on it. She needed to remember that above all else.

She deleted the reply and typed another.

Is there a dress code? What should I be wearing?

There now, that sounded less clueless, didn't it? Surely any woman would want to know that. But then the heavy weight sank into her sex and began to glow like a hot coal at the recollection of what she'd been wearing…or rather not wearing…when Ross had marched out of her room wearing nothing but a towel that morning.

And the innocent question suddenly seemed loaded with unintended innuendo.

'Oh, for the love of…'

She hissed, deleting the text. Then wrote another.

Cool, see you there.

She pressed 'send', before she could third-guess herself, and dumped the offending phone back on the paint table as if it were a grenade. Then she gathered up her brushes and palette so she could put aside her work for the day. She had two whole hours if she got a move on to scope out the cool little boutiques and vintage shops in the neighbourhood and find an outfit.

Something that made her look and feel good, but which also suited her own sense of style.

She swallowed, convulsively. At the very least her quest should help distract her for the next two hours from the panic still closing her throat and the hot rock now pulsing in her panties at the thought of seeing him again.

Hallelujah for neutral ground!

'Would you like another beer, sir?'

'No, I'm good.' Ross glanced at the waiter who had been hovering for the last ten minutes in the private terrace he'd hired in the chic roof-top restaurant—which was one of Manhattan's most popular eateries, apparently, not that he'd ever dined here before.

He winced slightly at how stunning the space looked with the sun setting on the horizon, casting a reddish glow over the dramatic view of Manhattan's skyline through the terrace's tall brick arches.

Terrific, the wait staff probably thought he was about to propose. When all he had wanted to do was to make absolutely sure they didn't give into the chemistry again before they got a few important things straight about his responsibilities to his son, and what any liaison between them while Carmel was in New York would and would not entail.

He cleared his throat. 'By the way, once

you've taken our drinks order, could you give us twenty minutes alone?'

'Absolutely, sir, and good luck,' the young man said, positively beaming. Ross bit back a groan.

But then Carmel appeared at the terrace entrance—and the groan got locked in his throat. The hum of arousal that had been tormenting him most of the day hit first, swiftly followed by what could only be described as awe.

He stood as she walked towards him.

Her vibrant red hair flowed out behind her in the light spring breeze, which also caught the floaty material of the short dress she wore, which was decorated with lavish red roses and clung to her torso, defining each and every one of the curves he had explored that morning.

A pair of combat boots and a leather jacket completed the original look. But as she approached his gaze rose to her face, and his pragmatism took another fatal hit. The make-up she wore—cherry-red lipstick to match the dress, smoky black eye liner and some kind of golden glitter on the lids, which sparkled in the light— made her look like a fairy queen, or a Valkyrie, stunningly beautiful, strikingly cool and so hot it hurt.

'Hi,' she said breathlessly as she reached him. 'Sorry I'm late. I wanted to walk the last couple of blocks.'

'Not a problem,' he murmured, trying to control the brutal reaction as he caught a lungful of her scent—something sultry and yet summery and as addictive as everything else about her.

'Wow, what a spectacular view,' she said, her voice rich with awe, the glittery eye shadow making her lids sparkle like rare gems.

There's only one spectacular view here, and it's not downtown Manhattan.

He swallowed round the lust swelling in his throat and held out her chair, silently cursing the decision to have this conversation in a restaurant.

Because the urge to lick every inch of her delicate flesh, taste the sweet sultry scent of her arousal, swallow the broken sobs of her pleasure again had already turned the hum of arousal into a roar.

'Is this a private space?' she said, glancing around.

He had to shake his head slightly, to unglue his gaze from her mouth and process the question.

Damn, De Courtney, get a grip.

'I thought you might prefer to talk without an audience,' he said.

Except talking is the last damn thing I want to do now.

He dragged his gaze away from those full lips.

Will her mouth taste like cherry?

'Really? That's so thoughtful of you,' she said, sounding as if she meant it as she seated herself. He walked back to his own chair and sat. He picked up his beer and finished it in one gulp to unstick his dry throat and give himself a moment to concentrate on easing the painful pulsing in his pants.

'More practical than thoughtful,' he said, desperately trying to regain his equilibrium and some semblance of control.

She blinked, the pure blue of her irises almost as breathtaking as the light blush on her pale skin.

'Thoughtful or not, I appreciate the privacy,' she said. 'I'm not gonna lie, I was nervous about meeting you here. I guess I'm too much of an unsophisticated Irish country lass to feel comfortable talking about my sex life over cocktails and cordon bleu cuisine with other people around.'

His gaze dipped of its own accord to the bodice of her dress, which cupped her breasts, the words 'sex life' delivered in that soft Irish burr detonating in his lap.

'You don't look unsophisticated,' he said. 'You look stunning.'

A bright smile curved her lips and lit her gaze, while the becoming blush spread across her collarbone. Something twisted deep inside him at the realisation of how much the offhand compliment had pleased her.

'Good to know the hour I spent scouring the vintage shops in Tribeca wasn't wasted,' she said as she shucked the leather jacket and handed it to the waiter, who had reappeared. The movement made the silky dress drift off her shoulder. The shot of adrenaline became turbocharged as he glimpsed a purple lace bra strap before she tugged the dress back up.

Just kill me now.

'Hiya,' she said to the waiter, who Ross noticed was staring at his date with his tongue practically hanging out of his mouth.

Possessiveness shot through him and he glared at the kid. 'Perhaps you'd like to take our drinks order?'

The young man jerked. 'Umm, yes, of course. What can I get for you, ma'am?' he said, not taking his eyes off Carmel. Apparently Ross had become invisible.

'What's good here?' she asked, and the waiter proceeded to stammer his way through a complex list of cocktails.

Ross's irritation increased.

What could only have been a few minutes but felt like several hours later, Carmel's new number one fan had finally left them alone together, as Ross had requested.

'So I take it you had a productive day,' he

said, struggling to make small talk—not his greatest strength at the best of times.

'Yes, very. Your apartment has so much light, it's a glorious place to paint,' she replied. 'And I'm particularly fond of my current subject. He's an adorable cockapoo with an abundance of personality. It's never hard to capture that on canvas. Plus, Nina dropped by to take Rocky out and we had a chat. She suggested introducing me to some of her other clients and their dogs while I'm here, which could be a great opportunity. She feels sure a lot of them would love a portrait of their pet.'

But I want you all to myself.

'I see,' he said, more curtly than he had intended, surprised by the strength of his disapproval. Where exactly was it coming from? Because it felt more than a little unreasonable... Just like the spike of possessiveness when he had caught the waiter staring at her. But he couldn't seem to shake it, even as the flushed excitement on her face dimmed.

'Do you have a problem with that?' she asked, the tone clipped as her smile died.

'Not precisely.' He shrugged, trying to make himself believe it. 'Obviously you're a free agent while you're here, and your career is your concern.' If painting pet portraits could really be called a career.

She'd had to drop out of art school to have his

child. It seemed her brother hadn't stepped in to offer her any financial support—which seemed callous in the extreme, given that the guy was a billionaire—but ultimately, Ross knew, Conall O'Riordan wasn't the one responsible for supporting her and his son, he was.

Suddenly his knee-jerk reaction made perfect sense. This wasn't about some Neanderthal desire to keep her all to himself as 'his woman' while she was here, it was simply his desire to right the many wrongs he'd done her, with his thoughtless reply to that text.

'Just so you know, I've worked out a generous maintenance package for you and Cormac with my financial team today, which means you won't have to continue shouldering the financial burden of his care any longer. Or, I hope, making compromises with your art based on that burden.'

Instead of her looking pleased with the news though, her brows drew down and those lush lips tightened into a thin line of disapproval. The blue of her irises turned to flame as outrage sparked in her eyes.

He braced himself for what he suspected was going to be a fairly spectacular argument. Discord was not something he usually enjoyed in a relationship. But as he watched her anger build, the arousal became razor sharp.

And it occurred to him that, unlike any other

woman he had ever dated, Carmel O'Riordan totally lived up to that age-old cliché, that she was even more stunningly beautiful when she was mad.

'Oh, have you now?' Carmel snapped, managing to temper her tone, just about.

But she could do absolutely nothing about the breathless rage threatening to blow her head off at his condescending and arrogant assumptions. And the prickle of fear beneath it. She'd spent the last four years refusing to take the many handouts Conall had offered her to help support her and Mac. So why should Ross's offer be any different?

His money didn't mean that he cared. She already knew that. So why should his persistence bother her so much? Or threaten to undermine the independence she'd worked so hard for?

'Since when has Mac become a burden to me?' she asked, because there were so many things wrong with his statement she didn't know where to start.

She knew she looked good in the fabulous vintage dress she'd found in a tiny shop off West Fourth Street, but still she'd been nervous at the thought of seeing him again, especially in the chic, uber-hip restaurant in the Murray Hill area of the city, which she'd immediately checked out on the Internet when the driver had told her of their destination. So nervous, in fact, she'd had to get out of the car a block early, even though she was already a few minutes late. Consequently, she'd been stunned…and moved…to find he'd booked this private space when she arrived, the view almost as staggeringly gorgeous as the sight of him in the twilight. His eyes had darkened, that searching gaze making bonfires ignite all over her skin, and the compliment had gone straight to her head. The nerves hadn't died, exactly, but they'd shifted, making her focus on *them*—and the rare chemistry that she was becoming increasingly sure she wanted to indulge.

Where was the harm in taking him up on his offer? If he could be pragmatic, why couldn't she? Her life was in Ireland after all, and his in New York. And while they shared a child, apart from Mac they had nothing else in common, having never shared more than a few hot, stolen moments together. She wasn't the artless, foolish, lovestruck girl she'd once been. She had believed herself in love once and it had all been a lie, based on chemistry and heat and one enchanting night. She wouldn't fall for that romantic nonsense again—that little wobble after they'd made love again was just that, nothing more than a wobble, an echo, of a girl long gone. This man had captivated her four years ago. But she knew now he couldn't be further from her ideal partner…

Surely his insulting offer of 'compensation' for her pain and suffering only confirmed that? So why couldn't she control the stupid emotion pushing against her ribs?

'I didn't say that,' he said, even though he'd said exactly as much.

'And if you'll recall I have never asked you for money,' she said, reiterating the point yet again, annoyed the fury she wanted to feel had become something a great deal more disturbing.

How could she be moved by his desire to support her—when she didn't want or need his support?

He leaned back in his chair, the appreciation in his gaze unmistakable. The top buttons of his shirt were undone, and the movement drew her gaze down to where his chest hair peeked out.

Heat settled like a hot brick in her belly, tangling with the nerves and the fury and the unwanted emotion to create a cocktail of sensations she seemed unable to extinguish.

'I know,' he said, the calm tone only adding to her agitation. 'You've been consistently clear on that point. But that doesn't mean I don't owe you for the upkeep of my son. And the things you have clearly sacrificed in the last four years.'

'I've sacrificed nothing I did not wish to sacrifice. And I'm perfectly happy with the life I have now,' she said. 'Maybe doing pet portraits seems like a waste of my talent to you, but I like it and I'm good—'

'I didn't say it was,' he cut her off.

'Yes, but you implied it,' she said, because he totally had.

But then he leaned forward and covered the fist she had resting on the table with his hand. 'I didn't mean to,' he said. 'I'm proud of you, and everything you've done to make a life for our child. But I remember the smart, witty, brilliant girl I met that night who captivated me with her dreams. You had ambitions for your future, which I destroyed. I want to give them back to you.'

The statement—delivered in that deep husky, forceful voice—cut off the outrage at the knees, the hot brick in her belly rising up to pulse painfully in her chest.

She tugged her hand out from under his as the fury disappeared to be replaced by the deep yearning she knew had no place in this relationship.

He felt beholden to her. She had to make it very clear to him, he wasn't. But why did the thought he would even want to give her back dreams that had died long ago seem so dangerous?

She shook her head, stupidly close to tears. He didn't understand that those dreams didn't matter any more, because he had given her some-thing far more precious. Making him understand that was what she had to concentrate on now.

'I don't want those dreams back,' she said. 'And I don't want your money, Ross. I thought I made that clear when I came here.'

He settled back in his chair, his gaze study-ing her with an intensity she remembered from that night—as if she were a puzzle he was de-termined to solve.

She'd found it exhilarating then. It scared her that look could still trigger the giddy bumps in her heart rate now.

She placed her hand in her lap, her skin still burning from the touch of his palm.

'As I understood it, you wanted me to form a relationship with Mac,' he said. 'I've said I'm willing to do that. I doubt I'll be much of a fa-ther, but I'm willing to try.'

'Okay,' she said.

'But you have to meet me halfway, Carmel. You have to let me provide financial security for you both.'

'Why?'

'Because it's important to me.'

'But *why* is it so important?' she asked again, almost as tired of his evasions as she was of her own see-sawing emotions.

He simply stared at her, but then he looked

away. And she knew he was debating whether to tell her more.

The waiter chose that precise moment to arrive with their drinks and the menus.

She spent several minutes checking the array of eclectic and delicious-sounding dishes, taking the opportunity to calm her racing heartbeat. But once they'd ordered and the waiter had left them alone again, she knew she had to find out why he was so obsessed with providing for her and Mac to stop herself from misconstruing his motivations again.

'You didn't answer my question,' she said.

He took a sip of the beer he'd ordered.

But just when she thought there was no way he would tell her more, he murmured, 'Because I spent my whole childhood watching my father exploit and abuse the women he slept with... And never live up to the responsibility of being a father to his own children. I vowed to myself then, I would be better than him.' He sighed, and for a moment she could see the turmoil in his eyes, devastating memories lurking there that she suspected he had no intention of sharing... 'What I did to you, and Mac, means I have broken that vow. Do you understand?'

Emotion pulsed hard in her chest at his forthright, honest answer. And the misery she glimpsed in his eyes.

It saddened her and moved her... But it also

made the fear release its grip on her throat. His offer, his need to provide for her wasn't really about her, about *them*. This was about his past, his childhood, his dysfunctional relationship with his father.

'You didn't exploit me, Ross. Or abuse me,' she said, knowing she couldn't let him take responsibility for her choices. Because it would make her a victim, and she never had been one. 'And you've offered to try and be a father to Mac, even though you're not confident in the role…' A lack of confidence she was beginning to understand now stemmed from his unhappy relationship with his own father. 'So you certainly haven't abandoned your responsibility towards him. And while it's touching you would want to give my dreams back to me, only I can decide what my dreams are, and only I can make them come true. The girl you met that night doesn't exist any more. She's not who I am now. And I'm glad of that. Having Mac has turned me into a stronger, smarter, less impulsive person. I was forced to grow up, for sure, but I've no regrets about that. And neither should you.'

He stared at her for the longest time, the silence only broken by the distant sound of sirens from the street below. She could feel her breath squeezing in her lungs, the moment somehow so significant—a battle of wills between his honour and her independence, which she knew she had to win.

But at last he broke eye contact and swore under his breath.

When his gaze met hers again, she saw rueful amusement, the feelings she had glimpsed earlier carefully masked again. But something had shifted between them, something important, because now she knew she had his respect.

'You're not going to accept the maintenance settlement, are you?' he said, giving it one last try, but he didn't seem surprised when she shook her head.

He thrust his fingers through his hair, which she had begun to recognise as a sign of his frustration, but then he let out a rough chuckle, which seemed to wrap around her heart. Why did she get the impression Ross De Courtney didn't laugh often enough?

'Do you have any idea how ironic it is that I wrote that unforgivable text four years ago convinced you were a conniving little gold-digger, and here I am now, frustrated beyond belief that you have point-blank refused—over and over again—to take the money I want to throw at you?'

She laughed, stupidly relieved they could finally share a joke about it. 'Actually, I'd call it poetic justice for that text, but then Conall has always said I've got a cruel sense of humour.'

'The fact I find myself agreeing with your brother only compounds the irony,' he said, the rueful tone intensified by the rich appreciation in his gaze.

Her heart bobbed into her throat. She swallowed it down ruthlessly, determined to concentrate on the pulse pounding in the sweet spot between her thighs, which he had exploited so comprehensively that morning—and nothing else.

'Doesn't it just?' she said, then wondered if she was enjoying the moment of connection a bit too much.

Whoa, girl. Don't go complicating this. Not again.

The sun had set on one of the most spectacular views she'd ever seen in her life, and it felt as if a huge hurdle to their future association as Mac's parents had been overcome. Plus she'd seen a crucial bit more about the man behind the mask. Maybe it had only been a glimpse, grudgingly given, but she could see now Ross's relationship with his father was the key to why he believed he would struggle to parent Mac, and she could give him some solace on that score at least, from her own experience. No need to make this new accord mean anything more.

'Would you let me at least set up a trust fund for Mac?' he said.

'I don't need your…' she began, but he held up his hand.

'I know you don't need my money,' he said. 'And I know now my money is no substitute for me attempting to be some kind of father to him. But it would make me feel a little bit better about abandoning him for the first three years of his life.'

She wanted to tell him no again. But she could see she needed to compromise now. Relinquishing even this much control over her son's life was hard, but how could she let Ross be a father to Mac, if she couldn't even allow him to set up a trust fund for his son?

'Okay, I can accept that,' she said. 'As long as you promise not to let him buy a motorcycle with the money when he's sixteen,' she added, desperately trying to make light of a difficult concession on her part.

She'd wanted Ross to consider being a real daddy to Mac. Why hadn't she realised, until this minute, everything that would entail?

He laughed. 'I'll tell my legal team to make his mother the primary trustee until he's thirty-five, how's that?'

'Perfect,' she said, just as the waiter arrived with the dishes they'd ordered.

The delicious aroma of grilled chicken and delicate spices filled her nostrils, and the tension that had been tying her gut in knots since getting his text that afternoon unravelled enough to make her realise she was absolutely ravenous.

Ross watched Carmel tuck into her food with the same take-no-prisoners gusto with which she appeared to tackle everything in her life—from motherhood, to art, to sex.

The woman certainly drove a hard bargain, he thought, as he sliced off a chunk of the succulent steak he'd ordered.

He let the juices melt on his tongue—while struggling to forget how much better she had tasted that morning. And how much he had been forced to reveal about his childhood, and his father.

He never talked about that time in his life. Or the man who had sired him. The flashbacks and nightmares he sometimes still suffered from were just one reason not to dwell on it. He'd had a disturbed night's sleep last night, thanks to the night terrors that had visited him in dreams and woken him up in a cold sweat—the shame of his own weakness almost as vivid as the brittle fear. But surely it was inevitable discovering he was a father would naturally bring the nightmares back again—at least for a little while.

Was that why he'd dived into a sexual relationship this morning that could effectively blow up in his face? Perhaps. But he was past caring about the consequences now. All he knew was that he had to have her again. But that still didn't stop him hating the pity in her eyes when he'd been forced to tell her the real reason providing for her and her son's financial needs was so important to him.

He tried to shrug it off as they finished their meal and talked easily about the day's business. Or easily enough, if you didn't count the ticking bomb in his lap ready to explode every time she licked the dark chocolate and sea-salt mousse off her spoon. Or he noticed that vintage dress slipping off her shoulder again and he got another glimpse of that damn bra strap.

As soon as she had licked the final drops of chocolate off her spoon, the waiter arrived to whisk their dishes away and offer them coffee. Ross waited patiently, or patiently enough, but when the waiter began to walk away, he opened his mouth to bring up the subject of their sleeping arrangements for the rest of the week when she beat him to the punch.

'My mother died when I was eight years old,' she said, her gaze fixed on his face.

'I'm sorry,' he said automatically, nonplussed not just by the complete non-sequitur but also the wealth of emotion in those bottomless sapphire eyes. And the twist of anguish in his gut, at the thought of her, as such a young child, losing her mother.

He ought to know how that felt—after all

he had lost his own mother when he was even younger… He tensed. Not true. Although his mother had died when he was five, he barely remembered her.

'It's okay, we weren't particularly close,' she said, still watching him with a disturbing level of intimacy.

'Are you sure?' he said, because he didn't believe her. He could hear the hollow tone of loss in her voice.

She gave him a weak smile. Then nodded. 'She suffered from depression. Had been battling it for all of my life—she had two miscarriages before I was born and that's when it struck. It got much worse when my daddy died in a farm accident. Then one Christmas morning, two years almost to the day of his death, she decided to end it. Con went to her room to wake her up… And found her dead.'

'Hell.' He whispered the word, shocked not just by the devastating picture she painted of her family's tragedy, but also the pragmatism with which she delivered the news. 'That's horrendous.'

'Yes…' She let out a small laugh completely devoid of humour. 'Yes, it is horrendous. For so many reasons. It's horrendous that my daddy died the way he did. It's horrendous that my mammy couldn't cope without him. It's horrendous she never got the help she needed. And that

Conall had to live with the trauma of finding her like that. And then had to take on so much responsibility when he was little more than a lad himself.'

'I'd say it's also horrendous you had to grow up without a mother,' he murmured.

'Yes, that too,' she said, almost as if her own loss was an afterthought. 'I suppose,' she added. 'But I didn't tell you so you'd feel sorry for me. I told you because…' She paused, sighed. 'Here's the thing—when I got pregnant with Mac my biggest fear was that I wouldn't be able to be a mother to him, because my own mother had been…' She hesitated again, then took a breath, and let it out slowly. 'Well, not much of a mother to me. I had no frame of reference. She hadn't been able to show love or even affection towards the end. She was in far too much pain to focus on anything other than the big black hole she couldn't climb out of. I worried constantly, while I watched my belly getting bigger, that I would have the same trouble bonding with my baby she had had bonding with me. Con and Imelda tried to explain to me it wasn't the same thing at all. That mam had been ill. But I'd always been secretly, even subconsciously, convinced there was something very wrong with me. And that's why she couldn't bond with me. That somehow I wasn't worthy of love. And what if that same thing was going to stop me loving Mac?'

He frowned. 'But that's absurd. What does one thing have to do with the other?' And anyway, he'd seen how she interacted with the boy. She obviously adored the child and he adored her. If anything, the closeness of their relationship had only intimidated him more.

'Nothing,' she said. 'Just like your father's inadequacies as a husband and a parent and, by the sounds of it, a human being have nothing whatsoever to do with you.'

He stared at her, the statement delivered in such a firm, no-nonsense tone, it took him a moment to realise they weren't talking about her family and her relationship with Mac any more. They were talking about him.

'That's not what I said,' he murmured, annoyed she had turned the tables on him so neatly, and annoyed even more by the fact he hadn't seen it coming.

'It's what you were thinking though,' she said.

Damn, she had him there.

'All I'm saying,' she said, leaning across the table to cover his hand with hers, 'is that it's okay to be scared of becoming a parent. Believe me, I was terrified. But don't let whatever cruel things he did to you influence your relationship with Mac. Because it's not relevant, unless you let it be.'

He stiffened and drew his hand out from

under hers. The empathy in her voice and the compassion in her gaze made his stomach flip.

'I never said he was cruel to *me*,' he murmured, even as the brutal memories clawed at the edges of his consciousness.

She watched him, her expression doubtful, but just when he thought she would call him out on his lie, her lips curved in a sweet and unbearably sympathetic smile. 'Then I'm glad.'

But he suspected she knew he wasn't telling the truth.

Reaching back across the table, he grasped her hand, then threaded his fingers through hers, suddenly determined to get back to a connection he understood.

She didn't resist, looking him squarely in the eyes. Her heartbeat punched her wrist as he rubbed his thumb across the pulse point.

'How about we stop talking about our pasts and start talking about what we plan to do for the rest of the night?' he said.

Being a parent was a role he doubted he would excel at for a number of reasons, but he was prepared to take her lead on that and hope for the best. Sex, however, was simple and something they both appeared to excel at, with each other. And it would defuse the tension currently twisting his gut into hard, angry knots.

'You didn't give me an answer,' he added, seeing the indecision in her eyes, which he was beginning to realise was unlike her. The woman seemed to have a natural inclination to rush headlong into everything. But not this. He wondered why that only made him want to convince her more.

'Because I haven't made up my mind,' she said, the words delivered on a tortured breath.

Smiling, as the shot of arousal echoed sharply in his groin, he opened her hand and lifted her palm to his mouth.

'Then let's see if I can persuade you,' he said, before biting gently into the soft flesh beneath her thumb.

She let out a soft moan, her vicious shiver of reaction making his own pulse dance.

But then she tugged her hand free and buried her fist in her lap. 'I want to sleep with you again,' she said boldly, her gaze direct. 'That's pretty obvious.'

'Ditto,' he said, unable to hide his grin as the dress slipped off her shoulder again.

She yanked it back up.

'I can see there's a but coming,' he said, determined to persuade her.

'But I don't want this…' She paused, and chewed her bottom lip, turning the trickle of heat into a flood. She thrust her thumb backwards and forwards between them. 'This *thing* between us to impact on your relationship with Mac.'

'It won't,' he said. 'Just to be clear, Carmel,'

he added, astonished to realise he had yet to give her the 'hooking up' speech he gave every woman—usually long before he slept with them. Why he hadn't got around to it until now with her was something he would have to analyse at a later date, but the first order of business was to remedy the situation.

'All we're talking about is a short-term arrangement for the duration of your stay. I don't do long-term, it's just not in my make-up.'

'I know,' she said, completely unfazed. 'Your sister said as much. Don't worry, I'm certainly not looking for long-term either. Especially not with a guy like you.'

He frowned, taken aback not just by her pragmatic reply but also by the spurt of annoyance. 'Katie said that?' he asked, not sure why his sister's candour felt like disloyalty.

Given the history of their sibling relationship, why would Katie say any different? And why should he care? But what the hell did Carmel mean by a 'guy like you'… What *kind* of a guy was he? Because he'd always considered himself fairly unique.

'Yes,' she answered. Then added, 'It's okay. Just sex works best for me, too.'

'Well, good,' he said, not quite able to keep the snap out of his voice as the annoyance and indignation combined. 'I'd hate to think you were expecting more from me than just orgasms on demand.'

Her gaze narrowed slightly. 'What's the problem? Isn't that the only thing you're offering?'

He forced himself to breathe and control the urge to contradict her... After all, it *was* all he could offer her, he'd just said so himself. It was all he had ever wanted to offer any woman.

But that didn't stop the questions queuing up in his head. Inappropriate questions which, intellectually, he knew he shouldn't want to ask her, had no right to ask her, but...

Who exactly had she slept with after losing her virginity to him? How many other men had there been in the past four years? Had they ever met his son? Formed a relationship with the boy when he had not? And what *kind* of guys *did* she consider worthy of more than just orgasm-supply duty? Because all of a sudden he wanted to know.

'Yes, precisely,' he said, through gritted teeth, holding onto the questions with an effort.

He'd get over his curiosity. This was just some weird reaction to spending all evening enthralled by those tantalising glimpses of her bra strap, the intermittent whiffs of her scent—fresh and sultry—and the torturous sight of her licking chocolate mousse off her spoon. Not to mention a much more revealing conversation about his past—and hers—than he had anticipated or was comfortable with. That was all.

She was still frowning at him. As if she was somehow aware he was struggling to keep his cool—which made the fact he was even more infuriating. What was it about this woman? How did she manage to push all his buttons without even trying? Buttons he hadn't even known he possessed till now…

No, he thought, that wasn't strictly speaking true. Because she'd pushed quite a few of his buttons that night four years ago, when he'd found himself haring after her escaping figure through the crowd of partygoers like a man possessed.

'So if orgasms on demand is all you want, what exactly is the problem with us going for it?' he managed, trying to finally ask a question that mattered, instead of all the ones that did not.

She heaved a deep sigh, which naturally made that damn dress slip off her shoulder again. Then glanced away from him. The fairy lights reflected in the glittery make-up on her eyelids. And he found himself catching his breath again, to stem the sharp flow of heat. She really was exquisite. This was all this was, an overpowering attraction to an extremely beautiful woman. Why was he complicating it? When he didn't want to and neither did she?

But then she turned towards him and he got momentarily lost in her sapphire eyes.

'I don't want it to be awkward, that's all. After it's over. Mac has to be my priority. As long as you're sure that won't be a problem?'

'A problem how?' he asked, because he was genuinely confused now.

'You know, that you won't get too attached. To me. And the orgasms.'

He wanted to laugh. Was she actually serious? Hadn't he just told her he didn't get attached? But the laugh died on his tongue, her dewy skin and large blue eyes suddenly making her look impossibly young… And vulnerable. When she'd never seemed that vulnerable before.

What a fool he'd been. He had been her first lover. And she was the mother of his child. Of course, that made her unlike any of the other women he had slept with, whatever her dating history since that night.

Not only that, but if he was to keep the promise he had made to her, about their son, he would never be able to sever this relationship the way he had severed every other relationship in his life before her when the woman he was dating had threatened to get too close.

For a moment, he considered forgoing the pleasure they could have during the coming days, and nights. To protect her, as well as himself, from the awkwardness she was referring to. But the rush of need came from nowhere, and he couldn't seem to say the words. Because it wasn't just sex he wanted, he realised. He wanted to know more about her. So much more.

He frowned, disturbed at how fascinated he was with her.

But surely, as long as he was well aware of the pitfalls of deepening this relationship over the next few days, he should be able to avoid falling into any of them?

After all, while he knew very little about real intimacy, so was naturally cautious about encouraging too much of it, he happened to be an expert at avoiding it.

'I guarantee, I won't get too attached,' he said, sure of this much at least.

And neither will you. Not when you realise how little I have to offer.

'Okay, then,' she said. 'I'd like to stay at your apartment for the rest of the week. And take you up on your orgasms-on-demand service.'

He gave a gruff chuckle, the rush of need making him a little giddy. He called the waiter over. 'Cancel the coffee order,' he said. 'And get the lady's jacket. We're leaving.'

CHAPTER TEN

CARMEL SHIVERED VIOLENTLY, but the cool spring breeze wasn't the only thing making goosebumps riot over her skin as the chauffeur-driven car drew up to the kerb in front of the restaurant entrance.

'Are you cold?' Ross asked, his hand settling on her back and making the silk of her dress feel like sandpaper.

She shook her head, aware of the heat slickening the heavy weight between her thighs.

She felt like that reckless girl again—intoxicated by the adrenaline rush. But she couldn't seem to stop herself from taking this opportunity to feed the hunger.

The driver opened the passenger door for them and Ross directed her into the warm interior. The scent of garbage from the street was replaced by the aroma of new leather and sandalwood cologne as Ross folded his tall body into the seat next to her.

'Put the partition up and take the scenic route, Jerry, slowly,' he said.

The hum of the screen lifting cocooned them into the shadowy space. She reached for her seat belt as the car pulled away, aware of her hand trembling. But as she went to snap the buckle in place, he caught her wrist.

'How about we live dangerously?' he said, the purpose and determination in his gaze accelerating her heartbeat.

She let the belt go, aware of the tension drawing tight in her abdomen, and the heat firing up a few thousand extra degrees.

She nodded, giving him permission to pull her up and over his lap.

Suddenly she was perched above him. Her hands on his shoulders, her legs spread wide, her knees digging into the soft leather on either side of him, the short silk dress riding up to her hips. Excitement rippled and glowed at her core, making the hot nub burn as his large hands captured her bottom to drag her down, until she settled onto the hard ridge in his pants. His fingers kneaded and caressed, as urgent, desperate desire pounded through her body. Every one of her pulse points throbbed in unison, the rhythm in sync with the painful ache at her centre. She rubbed herself against the thick ridge as he caught her neck, lifting the hair away to tug her face down to his.

He captured her moan, the kiss firm and demanding. Her lips opened instinctively, giving him greater access, letting his tongue drive into her mouth, exploring, exploiting.

A harsh groan rumbled up from his chest as he cradled her cheek and tugged her head back to stare into her eyes. 'Take off the jacket,' he said, or rather commanded.

She did as she was told, scrambling out of the garment. The dress fell off her shoulder, as it had done so many times during the evening, but when she went to yank it back up he murmured, 'Don't.'

His thumb trailed across her collarbone, rubbing over the frantic pulse, then slipped under her exposed bra strap to draw it off her shoulder with the dress. The material tightened, snagging on the stiff peaks of her nipples. He cursed softly and undid the buttons on the dress's bodice, his other hand still caressing her bottom, his thumb sliding across the seam of flesh at the top of her thigh.

She gasped, thrusting her hips forward, the contact too much and yet not enough, as she struggled to ride the ridge in his pants and release the coil tightening in her abdomen.

'Shh,' he murmured, the hint of amusement as rough and raw as she felt. 'We'll get to that in a minute.'

Just when she was gathering the words to

protest, the bodice of the dress fell open to her waist, revealing the purple lace bra. Then his devilish fingers delved behind her back. The sharp snap of the hook releasing moments later startled her.

'What the...?' she murmured, shocked by his dexterity, as she whipped her hands off his shoulders to catch her breasts before she exposed herself to the whole of Manhattan.

He chuckled again, the low sound more than a little arrogant. He ran his thumb under the heavy flesh, making her nipples tighten painfully. Then pressed his face into her neck, kissing, licking. With her hands trapped trying to preserve her modesty, she shuddered, forced to absorb the onslaught of sensation, his tongue and teeth cruising across her collarbone, his other thumb still gliding backwards and forwards across that over-sensitised seam—too close and yet not close enough to where she needed him.

'Let go of the bra, Carmel,' he murmured, his hot breath making her nipples hurt even more.

'I can't, I don't want everyone to see,' she managed, aware of the sparkle of lights outside as the car crossed the busy junction at Times Square and Broadway. 'We might get arrested.'

He laughed, apparently delighted by her gaucheness, the rat.

'The glass is treated. The only one who can see you is me.'

She shuddered again, his thumb dipping beneath the leg of her panties now, inching closer and closer to heaven.

'Are you…?' She swallowed around the lump of radioactive fuel suddenly jammed into her throat and throbbing between her legs. 'Are you sure?'

'Positive,' he said. 'Let go,' he demanded again.

Her hands released and seconds later he had pulled her arms out of the dress's sleeves, tugged her bra free and flung it away. She sat perched on his lap, naked to the waist, panting with need, but instead of covering herself, she forced herself to let him look his fill.

He groaned again, his gaze scorching the turgid flesh, before his hand cradled one heavy breast and his mouth captured the aching peak.

He licked and nipped, hardening the swollen flesh even more, making it pound and throb, before switching to the other breast. She had never realised she was so sensitive there. Her breasts had always been nothing more than functional. She'd loved feeding Mac when he was a baby, but this was so different, the arrows of need firing down to the hot spot at her core, building the brutal ache there with startling speed.

She cried out, barely able to breathe now

rs popped up, then his whole body

lopped over to the easel and stuffed
nto her belly. She rubbed his head,
ft laugh. 'Not interested, eh?'
going to miss Rocky almost as much
ster when she returned to Ireland to-

as she kidding? As much as she adored
she was going to miss Ross, so much
o much more.

anced at the sun beginning to slide to-
e New Jersey shoreline in the distance,
oil of her thoughts deepening.

shouldn't have happened. How had she
so attached to a moment—and a man—
was only supposed to be fleeting?
would be home soon from work—for
st night together.

body quickened. The last six days, ever
hey'd made their devil's bargain at the hip
y Hill restaurant, had gone by in a haze
sed emotions and insatiable desire.
ey made love two or three tim
, but why did it never seem to
ould even wake her each
ns, the heady touches trig
nstoppable response. They
of showering and eating breaki.

around the torturous sensations firing through her body. Cupping her bottom and lifting her slightly, he kept his mouth on her breasts, sucking, nipping, caressing, her sobs echoing round the car, and slipped his fingers inside her panties to find the slick seam of her sex.

She jolted, bowed back, as he touched the heart of her.

The moan built from her core, slamming through her as the orgasm ripped into her, firing up from her toes and cascading through her in undulating waves. She rode his fingers, panting, sobbing, every part of her obliterated in the storm of sensation.

At last the orgasm ebbed, releasing her from its grip.

She collapsed onto him, washed out, worn through, damp and sweaty, and shaking with the intensity of her pleasure, aware of her naked breasts pressed against the fabric of his suit jacket, the nipples wet and sore from his attention.

Damn, he was still fully clothed.

Perhaps she would have been embarrassed that she was virtually naked and draped over him like a limp dishrag, but she couldn't think about anything in the moment, her mind floating in a shiny haze somewhere between bliss and consternation.

The last throes of the orgasm rippled through

her as he finally slid his fingers from her swollen flesh. His hand caressed her neck, pressing her face into his shoulder, murmuring something in that deep, husky voice that made her feel cherished, important to him, when she knew she wasn't.

She clung on, breathing in the subtle scent of sandalwood and clean pine soap, the huge wave of afterglow at odds with the heavy weight settling on her chest.

How did he know just how to touch her, to make her fly? And how was she going to separate that from the painful pressure making her heartbeat stutter and stumble, and her ribs contract around her lungs?

He drew her head back at last, ran his thumb down the side of her neck as the car drew to a stop outside his loft. 'Ready for round two?'

She forced her lips to curve into what she hoped was a cocky grin, to cover the empty space opening up in her heart, then wriggled against the hard ridge in his pants while she pulled her dress back up. 'Bring it on.'

He laughed, but the sound reverberated in her chest, and did nothing to release the brutal stranglehold on her heart.

Rocky's ea
followed.
The dog
his snout
giving a s
She wa
as his ma
morrow.
Almost
Who v
the dog,
more. To
She g
wards th
the turn
This
become
which
Ross
their la
Her
since
Murra
confu
Th
night
He v
drea
and
habi

CHAPT

CARMEL DABBED THE br
last time, to add texture
lifted it away.

Enough. The portrait

She dropped the brush
shifted to glance past th
who had taken to floppin
stone floor every mornin
of the day with Nina.

Maybe he wasn't the pre
verse, but he had so much
risma she had been unable to
when she'd finished the portr
days ago.

And you want to give Ross s
to remember this week by.

She frowned, pushing aside
ught.

ley, boy, want to look at
the sadness—at the thoug
as nearly over—squeezin

in the mornings. And then he was gone for the day. The hours she spent without him seemed to stretch into an agony of panicked thoughts and painful longing, peppered with a ton of 'what ifs' which had become harder and harder to shut away when he returned from work each day. And then there was that brutal shot of exhilaration, excitement, when he came back—always with some delicious takeout food they could dive into before diving into each other—which had stopped being all about the sex days ago.

Why couldn't she stop thinking about him? Not just the things he could do to her body, but the way he looked at her when she spoke about her day, or about her latest video call with Mac, or about a thousand other minute details of her life—that look, as if he was truly interested in what she had to say about herself, about their son, had come to mean far too much too.

And that was before she even factored in all the questions she wanted answers to, but had become too afraid to ask. Because that would only increase the sense of intimacy—an intimacy she knew she shouldn't need, shouldn't encourage, but seemed unable to resist.

The truth was, the only thing anchoring her to reality for the last few days had been her work, and Mac. Her brave happy little boy still wasn't showing any signs of missing her much, Imelda insisting he went to bed without a problem each night and was having lots of fun not just on the farm but also at Kildaragh—with Katie and Con who, to everyone's astonishment given Con's love of a grand gesture, had decided to stay in Galway for the first couple of weeks of their honeymoon.

She would have to thank them both when she got home for allowing her three-year-old terminator to gatecrash their romantic break.

But even as she thought of Katie and Con, she felt the pang of jealousy too at the settled, happy, wonderful future they had ahead of them together.

What was that even about?

They deserved their happiness. And this interlude with Ross was never supposed to have a future, they'd agreed as much in the Murray Hill restaurant a week ago. She didn't even want a future with him. This stupid yearning was nothing more than fanciful nonsense... And probably way too much great sex. She'd become addicted to the endorphin rush, that had to be it.

She cleaned the brushes and draped a clean sheet over the portrait, which she had decided to present to Ross tonight as a parting gift.

Not a romantic gesture, simply an acknowledgement of the fun we've had over this past week.

She gulped down the raw spot in her throat, knowing it was past time to leave New York.

Mac had asked for the first time this morning when she was coming home, igniting the yearning she always felt when she was away from him. She needed to return to Ireland now—to her real life again. Her little boy missed her and she missed him. Desperately. He grounded her and gave her life strength and purpose.

The last week had been filled with the heady excitement she had craved as a girl—a conflagration of physical fireworks—which Ross seemed capable of igniting simply by looking at her a certain way—but with it had come the emotional roller coaster she remembered all too well.

She'd become way too invested in falling asleep each night in his arms, or sparring with him about everything from politics to rugby to the latest gala at the Met over a bowl of Lucky Charms in the morning, or their impromptu picnics on the roof terrace each evening—and that look, which made her feel special, cherished, important to him, when she knew she wasn't, not really.

The domesticity, the simplicity of their routine in the last week had given her a fake insight into what it might be like to live with this hot, charismatic and taciturn man for real—but he wasn't her man, and she didn't want him to be.

She huffed out a breath. As the week had worn on, and the evenings and the mornings they spent together had become more intense, she'd lost perspective, that was all, become that girl again, who wanted something she couldn't have. Just like the little girl before her, who had craved her mother's attention, her mother's love, precisely because it was unavailable. It was a self-destructive notion that she needed to get a handle on.

Even if this could have been more, she knew Ross wasn't right for her... He was still so guarded, so wary, so unwilling to open himself to her or anyone else, but it horrified her to think that might be why she was so attracted to him. He presented a challenge, and she'd always had a bad habit of taking on challenges she couldn't win.

Rocky barked and shot out into the living area. Her heart thundered into her throat at the sound of the apartment's door opening, and the excited yips as Rocky gave his master his customarily insane greeting.

He's back early.

She held her ground, swallowed past the ball of anguish in her throat and finished putting away her paints, holding back the foolish urge to run out and give Ross an equally enthusiastic greeting.

Don't go soft now. Be cool, be calm, be smart. Protect yourself. Tonight's your last night... This is the way it has to be...

But as she listened to Ross's low voice talking to his pet and then he shouted, 'Hey, Carmel, where are you?' her heart ricocheted against her chest wall like a cannonball and the surge of sensory excitement was followed by the deep-seated yearning she still had no clue how to ignore.

She walked out into the living area, her thundering heart lifting into her throat as she spotted him, tall and indomitable and so hot in his business suit, with one hand caressing the dog's head and the other ripping off his tie.

His gaze locked on hers, possessive and intense—as always. And the heady rush of adrenaline and need shot through her on cue.

'Hey, how are you?' she said, disconcerted when her voice broke.

'Good,' he said. 'Now I'm finally home.'

The word *home* echoed in her chest, with far more resonance than she knew it deserved.

This isn't your home, or Mac's, it's his—he doesn't want you here, not in the long term. Why can't you get that through your eejit head?

'Sit, Rocky,' he demanded in a voice that brooked no argument. The dog planted his butt on the floor, his tail swishing against the polished wood, as Ross marched past him towards her.

Grasping her chin, he lifted her gaze to his, and the need on his face stabbed into her gut.

'Let's go to bed.'

It wasn't really a question, but she nodded anyway, the sensation flooding her system helping her to ignore the pulse of longing beneath.

He boosted her into his arms and strode across the room towards the curving metal staircase in the middle of the large space. She wrapped her legs around his waist and kissed him hungrily, channelling all the yearning into the promise of release.

Sex will make this better. Sex will take this ache away. Because sex is all this was ever meant to be.

But as they crashed into his bedroom together, and began to rip off each other's clothes, the brutal pain in her chest—and the frantic feeling of desperation and confusion and need—refused to go away.

Ross drew out slowly, the last spasms of another titanic orgasm still pulsing through his system as her swollen flesh released him. He rolled off her, flopped down, exhausted, sated— or as sated as he could be when he didn't seem able to completely satisfy his endless craving for her. He covered his eyes with his arm, holding back a staggered groan.

He could hear her breathing beside him, her deep sighs as shattered as he felt.

He'd taken her like a madman. Again. Hadn't

even had the decency to wait until they'd eaten. Hell, he hadn't even been able to stop on the way home tonight long enough to pick up take-out for their evening meal, the way he'd been forcing himself to do up to now—just to prove he could be civilised enough to feed her before jumping her.

Why did this hunger keep getting worse? More insistent? Why couldn't he stop thinking about her? All day. Every day.

He'd lost focus at work in the last week, stopped caring about most of it, had curtailed his standard fourteen-hour days to eight hours, because he couldn't bear to be away from her a minute longer.

Today he'd been caught daydreaming about the sound of her sobs in the shower that morning while doing a conference call about a container ship emergency in the Gulf of Mexico—and made a fool of himself in front of the head of De Courtney's South American division and her two assistants because he'd had absolutely no clue what they were discussing when she asked him a direct question.

But as his breathing finally evened out and his heartbeat slowed, he knew it wasn't just this insatiable hunger that was the problem. It was so much more.

It was the sight of her each morning, her long legs crossed as she perched on one of the stools at his breakfast bar and tucked into the cereal she'd become as addicted to as he was.

It was the soft glow that seemed to light up her face every time she told him some new story or detail about their son—a soft glow he had become addicted to as well. So addicted he wasn't even sure any more if it was the insights she was giving him about his son—such as his obsession with horses and dogs, his love of arranging his toys in long lines all over her living room, his hatred of eating anything green despite her attempts to hide it in everything she cooked for him—which fascinated and captivated him, or the joyous light in her eyes when she was talking about Cormac.

It was the feel of her—so warm and soft in his arms as he fell asleep each night—that had managed to chase away the nightmares.

It was the dabs of bright colour in her hair from her work, which he enjoyed washing out after they had made love, the smell of turpentine and oil paint that lingered on her, and around the apartment now.

It was even the thought of knowing she would be there in the evening, waiting with Rocky, when he got back from the office. Making him realise he'd never really considered his condo a home until this week—which was ludicrous, seeing as he had owned the duplex loft for over six years, ever since moving to Manhattan.

But worst of all, it was the knowledge of how much he was going to miss all those things when she left tomorrow morning.

She stirred beside him and sat up. 'Did you bring anything home for supper?' she asked.

He dropped his arm, the inevitable hunger resurfacing as he absorbed the sight of her naked back, his gaze drifting down to her buttocks. 'Not today,' he said, unable to stop himself reaching out to caress the soft swell. She shivered and he lifted his fingers, aware of the heat settling in his groin again. 'I've run out of ideas. We've tried out pretty much every place I usually use,' he lied to cover the truth—that he hadn't wanted to wait a moment longer than necessary to see her again. 'How about I take you out for supper?' he made himself ask, even though the last thing he wanted to do right now was leave the apartment. Or this bed.

The truth was, if he could, he would happily spend the next fourteen hours, before her flight home, buried deep inside her, losing himself in this incendiary physical connection so he wouldn't have to dwell on all the other things he was going to miss when she was gone. And the powerful urge to ask her to stay a while longer. He'd even come up with a plan to make that happen. Had asked his assistant to rearrange his schedule and have the staff at his estate in Long Island open up the house, simply so he could take a whole week off for the first time since his father's death ten years ago.

But he'd nixed the idea on the way home.

When the hell had he become so obsessed with her? It would be laughable, if it weren't so damn disturbing. And would it really be wise to spend twenty-four hours a day with her, when he was already spending every waking minute thinking about her?

She glanced over her shoulder at him, holding the duvet up to cover her breasts, breasts he had just spent several insatiable minutes devouring because he knew exactly how sensitive they were—and how she loved his attention there. A warm flush highlighted the freckles that covered her nose. Funny how he found the surprising glimpses of modesty as captivating as everything else about her. It enchanted him, probably because it reminded him so forcefully of the girl he had met that first night. The girl she had insisted was long gone. The girl who had been bold and beautiful, brutally honest and artlessly arousing, and yet at the same time had an innocence, a fragility beneath the boldness that had captivated him then, and made him want to protect her now... Even though he was fairly sure the only person she needed protecting from was him.

She smiled, that quick, generous smile that always made his heartbeat bounce in his chest.

'Okay, that would be grand. I've not seen much these past few days except the inside of this apartment,' she said. The little dig made him laugh, but he could see something else in her eyes that had his bouncing heart swelling in his throat.

'But I've got something to show you first,' she added, then threw off the duvet and got off the bed.

She hunted around for her clothing as he watched her, unable to deny himself the simple pleasure of studying her as she dressed in quick, efficient movements. First her panties went on, then the bra, which she hooked in the front then swivelled round so she could loop the straps over her shoulders. She wiggled back into the faded jeans—speckled with paint—which he knew she wore while she worked, then threw on a baggy green T-shirt with the insignia of the Irish Rugby Union Team, which was speckled with even more paint.

He stretched, and adjusted himself, grateful the heavy duvet hid the insistent erection already making a second appearance.

Since when had he found watching a woman dress so hot?

She swept back her wild red hair and tied it into a knot behind her head, then looked over her shoulder. 'You'll have to get out of bed, you know, if you're to see your surprise… And we're to eat before midnight.'

He chuckled, her sharp tongue as alluring as the rest of her. And forced himself to sit up. 'I'm going to have a quick shower. Do you want to join me?'

Arousal darkened her eyes, but she shook her head. 'If I do that we'll never get out of the apartment and you know it.'

'True,' he said, trying to keep his voice light and unconcerned, despite the brutal pulse of disappointment and yearning. And the knowledge that he was even going to miss her attitude.

Time to back off, De Courtney. This obsession is getting out of hand.

He dropped his feet off the bed, keeping the duvet firmly over his lap.

'I'll shower downstairs and meet you in the atrium,' she said, rushing out of the room before he could change his mind, and attempt to seduce her back into his bed.

He took care of the insistent desire in the shower—while he tried not to dwell on the humiliating fact he hadn't had to resort to such antics since he was a desperate teenager in an all-boys boarding school in the Scottish Highlands and the chance to interact with girls had been rarer than the chance to interact with Martians.

He took his time shaving and getting dressed

in more casual clothes, determined not to let the yearning get the better of him again. Perhaps it was a good thing Carmel was leaving tomorrow. He'd become fixated on her, that much was obvious. Establishing his relationship with his son was what mattered now. Avoiding hard conversations about that had been all too easy while he was focussed on feeding the hunger—perhaps that was why it had resolutely refused to be fed.

He finally made his way downstairs. Rocky greeted him with his usual over-the-top enthusiasm. 'Hey, fella,' he said, his voice strangely raw as he knelt down to give the hound a tummy rub.

Thank God for the dog. He'll keep me company when she's gone. I'll be fine.

He'd never had any trouble being alone before now. This was all in his head.

But then he walked into the atrium and saw her standing in front of her easel, the evening light turning her damp red hair to a burnished gold. And the yearning dropped into his stomach like a stone.

I don't want her to go. Not yet. I'm not ready. And there's the boy to consider, I need to meet him, but I need her help with that.

Then she turned and stepped aside. 'Here, what do you think?' she said, directing his gaze to the painting on the easel beside her. 'I thought you might like a portrait of Rocky.'

He stared, so stunned for a moment, he was

utterly speechless. The portrait was exquisite of course, the likeness striking, the dopey adoration in the dog's expression so expertly captured, it was hard to believe his pet wasn't embedded in the canvas instead of by his side, busy licking the back of his hand.

But as his gaze met hers, again, it wasn't the exquisite artistry of the portrait—the evidence of her incredible talent—that had the stone in his stomach turning into a boulder the size of El Capitan.

'You painted that? For me?' he said, the boulder rising up to scratch against his larynx. So astonished, he could barely speak.

He couldn't remember the last time he had received a gift. His father had never been a gift giver—believing his son's birthdays were simply another chance to drum into him his responsibility to the De Courtney name, while his Christmases had always been spent at school as a child. He didn't currently have any friends close enough to know when his birthday was, let alone celebrate it with him. Plus he avoided dating over the holiday season simply to avoid the kind of sentimentality that was now all but choking him.

Not only was this gift rare, though, it was also so thoughtful.

How had she captured what he saw in his pet so perfectly? Did she know how much he relied on Rocky for the warmth and companionship he had convinced himself he didn't need?

And suddenly he knew. He couldn't let her go. Because he needed time to find a way back from the precipice he was standing on the edge of as she stared at him now with the same soft glow he had seen on her face when she talked about their son… And the yearning in his chest turned into a black hole.

'Ross? Is everything okay?' Carmel's heart slammed into her throat. He looked stricken, his gaze jerking to hers—the flash of panic in it disturbing her almost as much as the melting pain in her own heart as she absorbed his visceral and transparent reaction to her gift. One minute he'd been his usual guarded self, his defences very much back in place, as she knew they would be, because they always seemed to return after they made love. She would glimpse something in the throes of passion that she had become as addicted to as the endorphin rush of good, hard, sweaty sex. But as soon as they collapsed on top of each other, each joining more frantic and furious than the last, the mask would return, and she was sure she had imagined that intense moment of connection.

But as his gaze rose to hers now, and she watched the shutters go down again, she knew she hadn't imagined it this time. Because for one terrifying moment he had been totally transparent and what she'd seen had broken her heart—yearning, desperation, confusion and panic, but most of all need.

And in that split second, she had the devastating thought that she was falling in love with him. That this yearning wasn't about sex, or the unfulfilled needs of that emotionally abandoned little girl, it was so much more dangerous than that.

'Do you like it?' she asked, her voice raw, terrified that her heart was already lost to him and knowing that, even if it was, it didn't really change anything. Because he had given her no indication that his heart was available to her. Or would ever be. That he was even capable of ever letting down the guard he had built around it.

Maybe he could love his dog. A dog's love was unconditional, and uncomplicated. But what indication had he given her he could love her? Or that he was even willing to try? None whatsoever.

She'd spent her childhood beating her head against that brick wall—trying to make her mother love her—and it had made her into someone reckless and impulsive and ultimately afraid. She couldn't spend her adulthood doing the same with him. But even knowing that, she couldn't seem to stop the giddy rush of pleasure when he spoke again, his voice rich with awe.

'It's incredible.'

'I thought I could give it to you as a parting gift,' she said, determined to remember their time was nearly over. She couldn't give into this yearning, this hope, this foolish need. Not again.

'Don't go.'

'What?' she asked, sure she hadn't heard him correctly. Wishing she hadn't felt her heart jolt.

'Don't go back to Ireland tomorrow,' he said. 'I have an estate in Long Island, which I mostly use for occasional weekend breaks and business hospitality purposes. But I haven't taken a proper holiday in ten years. The forecast is for warm weather. I'd like to take you there.'

'I can't stay,' she said, upset that for a second she'd even considered accepting his invitation. How far gone was she, that she would even want to pursue a reckless pipe dream when she'd missed her little boy so much? 'I need to go home. Mac needs me. And I need him.'

To ground me again and make me realise this isn't real.

'I thought we could fly him over, so he could spend the time with us there.'

'Are you...? Are you serious?' she asked, so shocked by his suggestion she couldn't think over the pounding in her chest.

He'd listened when she'd regaled him with stories about Mac, had asked a lot of questions about their child, but she hadn't expected this.

'Absolutely. If I'm going to form a relationship with him, I think we both know I'm going to need your help. I know nothing about children. This is a big step for us all. I don't want to make a mistake.'

'That's… I'm overwhelmed,' she said, because she was. But she forced the foolish bubble of hope down—knew it had no place in this arrangement. She needed to be practical now… And most of all she needed to protect herself, not just from these foolish, fanciful notions about Ross and her, but from the devastating prospect of letting that insecure girl reappear again, who had thought she could make someone love her just by wanting it enough.

'I'd have to go back and get him,' she said. If they were going to do this thing, it had to be about Mac—not them. Because there was no them. 'He's only three, I couldn't send him over on his own.'

'How about I ask Katie if she will accompany him?' he said. 'I need to repair things with her anyway. It's been five years and, after my behaviour at the wedding, I think perhaps more than a ten-minute conversation is required.'

Again, she was surprised, at his willingness to consider such an option. And at how open he was being to having a proper conversation with his sister. Surely this was a huge sign he was willing to do much more than simply go through the motions in his relationship with Mac?

'Okay, that could work,' she said, not sure Katie would go for it—after all, she was on her honeymoon at the moment. If anything, she was fairly sure Conall would insist on using the Rio Corp jet and accompanying his wife to New York, but if Ross was serious about repairing this rift, he would eventually have to talk to Con too. And involving her brother and his wife would be a good way of helping her to keep things in perspective and focus on what mattered now—Ross forming a relationship with his son.

'Good, I'll make the arrangements,' he said, in his usual no-nonsense fashion. But then he stepped forward and cupped her cheek. 'How about we order takeout? I'm not sure I want to leave the apartment tonight.'

She made herself smile, but the gesture felt desperately bittersweet as her abdomen pulsed at the purpose in his gaze. She covered his hand with hers, to draw it away from her face. 'That would be good, but, Ross...' She swallowed, knowing she had to make a clean break from him and the intimacy they had shared, before their son arrived. The danger to her heart was all too apparent now. 'We can't continue sleeping together while Cormac is with us. It would confuse him.'

It was a cop-out. Cormac wouldn't be confused. He didn't need to know they were even sleeping together if they were discreet. A part of her hated the lie and using her son to reinforce that lie. But she had no choice. Not if she was to keep her heart secure for the week ahead. Watching Ross bond with his son would be hard enough, without introducing the intimacy they had already shared into the equation. An intimacy she hadn't been as good at dealing with as she had believed.

'Why?' he asked. 'Hasn't he seen you dating before?'

'No, there hasn't been anyone…' She stopped. But his eyes narrowed, his gaze seeing much more than she wanted him to see. The flush burned in her cheeks, but it was already too late to disguise the truth.

Damn my Irish colouring.

'There hasn't been anyone but me?' he asked.

She could lie again. She wanted to lie, only feeling more exposed and wary at what the truth revealed, aware of the sudden intensity in his gaze. But a bigger part of her knew lying would only give the truth—that he was the only man she had ever slept with—more power.

She shrugged, even though the movement felt stiff. 'Being a single mum is a full-time job. I haven't had the time,' she said, trying to make it seem less of a big deal. Knowing in her heart it was just more evidence of how careful she needed to be now.

She had expected him to look spooked by the admission. Would have welcomed that reaction—because it would have given her at least some of the distance she so desperately craved.

But instead of looking spooked, he just looked even more intense. So intense she could feel the adrenaline rush over her skin.

'I see,' he murmured, then framed her face and pulled her close.

He slanted his lips across hers, his tongue thrusting deep, demanding a response. A response she was powerless to stop. The kiss was raw and possessive, and heartbreakingly intense.

She held his waist and kissed him back, letting the fear go, to indulge in the moment.

She wasn't that reckless girl any more. She would never jeopardise Mac's happiness, or her own, on a pipe dream—which was why she couldn't sleep with him again after tonight.

But as he lifted her easily into his arms to carry her upstairs she groaned, and gave herself permission to indulge that reckless girl, one last time.

CHAPTER TWELVE

'THANK YOU FOR interrupting your honeymoon, Katie. And bringing Mac over,' Ross said as he headed towards the liquor cabinet, needing a stiff drink. The evening sunlight shone off the water in the distance, the scent of sea air helping to calm his racing heartbeat.

He'd held his son for the first time ten minutes ago. His hands shook as he lifted the whisky bottle and splashed a few fingers in his glass.

'You're welcome, Ross. He was extremely excited during the flight over. But I think it was all too much for him and he crashed out on the helicopter ride to the estate,' Katie said.

He'd forgotten how little his child was. When the helicopter had touched down at the Long Island estate's heliport twenty minutes ago and his brother-in-law had emerged from it with Ross's sister by his side, carrying the sleeping boy— the child had looked so small and defenceless Ross's ribs had tightened.

Cormac had woken up momentarily, and

smiled sleepily at his mother, reaching out to be held. She had scooped him into her arms with practised ease—but then she'd turned to Ross and said, 'He's heavy. Do you want to hold him?'

He'd reached to take the boy, only realising as he lifted the sleeping child into his arms that he had no idea what he was doing.

But Mac had settled his head against his shoulder without complaint, his small arms wrapping around Ross's neck—the sweet scent of talcum powder and kid sweat invading his senses as the child dropped back into sleep.

Ross's heartbeat had accelerated as a boulder formed in his throat. Part panic, part fear, but mostly a fierce determination that he would do anything to protect this child. It had reminded him a little of how he had felt when he had lifted Rocky as an injured and abused puppy out of that dumpster, but this time the feeling had been a thousand times more intense.

But that moment had also brought the reason why he had invited Mac…and Carmel to Long Island into sharp and damning focus.

He took a gulp of the fiery Scotch, let the liquor burn his throat to suppress the jolt of annoyance at the memory of the assessing look in Conall O'Riordan's eyes as he had lifted the boy back out of Ross's arms so he and Carmel could settle him in his new bed, while Ross and Katie talked.

The knowledge O'Riordan had effectively taken Ross's place in Cormac's life for the last three years had been a sobering thought. But what was worse was the knowledge he had no right—not yet—to stake any kind of claim to being the boy's father. And that his reasons for inviting the boy here—with his mother—had been far from altruistic.

He'd resented Carmel's suggestion they stop having sex yesterday evening, had been filled with an almost visceral urge to change her mind, especially when she had told him he was the only man she had ever slept with. That swift surge of possessiveness, of ownership almost, had made their joining even more intense, even more desperate, but this afternoon when they'd arrived at the estate—and this evening when they'd waited together for O'Riordan's helicopter to arrive—he'd forced himself to back off. To give her space. And now—after holding his son for the first time—he realised that attempting to seduce her back into his bed would be a mistake.

He'd waited far too long to take on the responsibility of parenthood. He could not afford to mess it up. But more than that, what more did he really have to offer Carmel?

He splashed another finger of Scotch into a tumbler. 'Would you like something to drink, Katie?'

'Nothing for me, thanks,' his sister said, but then he noticed the flush on her cheeks, and the way her hand swept down to cover her stomach.

He frowned, his gaze meeting hers. 'My God, you're pregnant.'

The colour intensified, and her eyes widened. 'How did you know?'

He choked out a laugh, the stunned surprise on her face somehow helping to break the tension gathering in his stomach.

It made him remember how transparent she'd always been. Even as a lonely, grief-stricken teenager, the first time he'd met her. She'd run up to him that day—a complete stranger—and wrapped her arms around him, her eyes flooding as she told him how grateful she was to have a brother.

He could remember at the time being extremely uncomfortable. Patting her stiffly on the shoulder and wondering what the hell he was supposed to do with a grieving teenage girl who he did not know from Adam.

In the end, he'd abrogated the responsibility to a series of expensive boarding schools. He'd failed Katie that day. He couldn't afford to fail Mac in the same way. Surely that was where he had to concentrate his energies, not on the kinetic sexual connection he shared with the boy's mother, however tempting.

'You're an open book, Katie,' he said.

The knots in his stomach tightened again as the news of her pregnancy echoed in his chest.

His baby sister was having a baby of her own. But how much better prepared for that role was she than he was? Katie, even as a girl, had always been open and compassionate and generous. All things he would have to learn, if he was going to have any hope of living up to the task of being a father.

'Or you're a mind reader,' she countered, sounding disgruntled.

He smiled and poured her a soda water, added ice and a slice of lime. He handed her the drink. 'I guess congratulations are in order. When is the baby due?'

She took the glass and grinned, all the love she already felt for this unborn life shining in her eyes. 'We had the dating scan two days ago and they basically put the due date on Christmas Eve,' she said, her excitement suffusing her whole face now. 'Dreadful timing really— who wants to be born on Christmas Eve? But we got pregnant quicker than we thought. Poor Con's still in shock, actually. He was convinced it would take several months—he had worked out a whole schedule for when exactly we should stop taking contraception so we'd have a spring baby, which he thought was the perfect time for a birthday.' She cradled her still flat belly, her grin widening. 'But apparently baby didn't get the memo.'

'Bummer,' he said, his smile becoming genuine at the thought of 'poor Con' having his carefully laid plans shot to hell.

Welcome to the chaos, bro.

But then the empty space opened up again.

When was his own son's birthday? How could he even pretend to be a father when he didn't know something so fundamental…and had never thought to ask?

'You should have told me you were pregnant,' he said, as it occurred to him she hadn't just changed her honeymoon plans to make the trip to the US at such short notice. 'Carmel and I could have made other arrangements.'

'Don't be silly, I'm perfectly fine,' she said, touching his arm. 'And we were happy to do it. Con has a house in Maine he's been waiting to show off to me for a while and then we're heading to his place in Monterey.'

He very much doubted her husband had been quite as happy to accommodate him—as he recalled the frown on O'Riordan's face when he'd first spotted Carmel and him standing together at the heliport.

He suspected the guy was even now grilling Carmel about what exactly the two of them had been doing together in the last week, but he kept his opinion of O'Riordan's reaction to himself, the enthusiasm in Katie's eyes both humbling, and painfully bittersweet—because his affair with Carmel was now over.

'I'm so excited you've made the decision to be a part of Mac's life. He's an incredible little boy. You won't regret it,' she added.

'I just hope he doesn't,' he mumbled.

'He won't,' Katie said and touched his arm. 'I think you're going to make an incredible father.'

'Thanks,' he said, humbled all over again by her belief in him, as it occurred to him he'd done absolutely nothing to deserve it.

The truth was he'd been a piss-poor brother. And it was way past time to change that too. *Really* change it.

'I'm sorry, Katie,' he said, realising how long overdue the apology was when she tilted her head, her gaze puzzled, her smile fading.

'What for?' she asked softly.

'Everything.' He huffed out a breath, looked away, because he couldn't bear to see the scepticism he knew he *would* deserve.

His gaze tracked towards the horizon, across the manicured lawn, the tennis courts, the guest house where Carmel and Mac would be staying, the pool—surrounded now by new railings, which he'd had installed before Mac's arrival.

He'd spent a small fortune refurbishing the estate buildings three years ago—the mansion had originally been constructed by a railroad baron in the nineteen-tens but had fallen into disrepair since the eighties. But how much time had he spent here? Virtually none. In many ways, the lavish but unlived-in property was a symbol for his life. He'd worked so hard, spent so much time and effort building De Courtney's, but with every goal he had achieved his life had only become emptier as he'd shed all his personal responsibilities, and shunned companionship and love.

The L word made him shudder.

Did he love his son? Already? Was that possible? The thought had his heart rate ramping up again.

He breathed deeply, trying to counter his haphazard pulse.

Calm down. You can handle this.

The twinkle of lights from the pool house reflected off the surface of the water as the sun sank into the ripple of surf in the distance, casting a red glow over the wooden walkway that tracked past the tennis courts and into the dunes. Whatever happened now, whatever he was capable of feeling for the boy, he made a vow never to shirk his responsibilities again. He would learn to be a good father. And maybe finally fulfil the promise he had made all those years ago to be a better man than his own father.

And he would keep his hands off Carmel, even if it killed him.

He turned back to his sister. 'I'm sorry for treating you like an inconvenience, a debt to be paid, rather than a sister,' he said in reply to her question.

She stood, watching him. But, weirdly, he didn't see scepticism, all he saw was compassion.

'You deserved—needed—so much more than I was ever capable of giving you. So I'm sorry for that too,' he finished.

She shook her head. But the all-inclusive smile, the unconditional love he knew he did not deserve, still suffused her features—and tore a hole in his chest.

'You did the best you could, Ross. But I also think you're capable of much more than you think,' she said, so simply it had fear slicing into his heart.

No, he wasn't. He knew he wasn't. He was selfish and entitled and absolutely terrified of love... Or he would have been a much better brother to her all those years ago.

And he would never have asked his sister to bring his son all the way to America, primarily so he would have a chance to sleep with the boy's mother for another week.

'I think you're ready now to open your heart to Mac...' Her smile widened, her eyes twinkling with excitement. 'And maybe his mum too, because it's pretty obvious there's a lot more going on between you and Carmel than just figuring out your new parenting arrangements.' She laughed, the sound light and soft and devoid of judgement. 'And that makes me so happy. Carmel's an amazing woman, brave and honest and talented and…' Her smile widened. 'Well, I'll stop being a matchmaker, but I think you two could make a great couple—even without factoring in Mac.'

'I'm not sure your husband agrees,' he managed as the shaft of fear twisted and turned in his gut.

Maybe he could love his son. He already felt the fierce need to protect him. But Carmel? That wasn't going to happen. Ever.

'Ignore Conall,' Katie said, still beaming, still so sure he would make a good partner for Carmel… On no evidence whatsoever.

Katie wasn't just sweet, and generous and kind, he realised, she was also irrepressibly optimistic and hopelessly naïve. Why else would she have forgiven him so easily after the way he'd treated her?

'My husband has been known to be chronically wrong about affairs of the heart,' she continued, the secret smile tugging at her lips suggesting her courtship with O'Riordan hadn't been quite as blissful as Ross had assumed.

Yeah, but O'Riordan's dead right about this.

'And he's more like a father to Mel and Immy

than a brother,' she added. 'So he has a tendency to be a tad overprotective. But, believe me, Carmel is her own woman. And if she trusts you enough to let you form a relationship with Mac, my guess is she's probably already halfway in love with you.'

The guilt plunged like a knife deep into his gut.

No way. She can't be in love with me.

'I see,' he said, taking another sip of his whisky as he hoped like hell Katie was wrong.

CHAPTER THIRTEEN

'MR ROSS, CAN WE play more?'

'No way, slugger, it's time to get out of the water before you turn into a fish.'

Carmel grinned as she listened to Ross and Mac in the pool. Her little boy giggled and she lowered her book to see Ross hoist Mac out of the water—where they'd been playing together all afternoon—and sling him over his shoulder to stride out of the pool.

Rocky joined in the fun, barking uproariously and dashing over from his spot beside Carmel's lounger. Ross stood on the pool tiles—the water running in distracting rivulets down his broad shoulders and making his swimming shorts cling to his backside.

The inevitable endorphin rush joined the painful pounding in her chest that was always there when she watched the two of them together.

She blinked, her skin heating—her heart hurting in ways she hadn't expected and couldn't afford to acknowledge.

Ross lowered the giggling, squirming Mac to his feet, and she found herself enchanted by the tableau they made together. He wrapped a towel around his son and began to dry him with a confidence she was sure would have surprised them both six days ago—when she had handed him their sleeping son at the heliport, and she had seen the stunned emotion as he'd held Mac for the first time.

Mac's giggles got considerably louder as the dog helped out with the drying routine using his tongue.

'Rocky, sit!' Ross said.

The dog stopped licking Mac's face and planted its butt on the tiles—having learned to obey his master's voice. Mac wrapped his arms round Rocky's neck, burying his face in his fur.

'I love Rocky,' he said.

The dog sat obediently. Any worries they'd had about introducing Rocky to their child had quickly been dispelled. The pressure on her chest increased. The rescue dog had turned out to be a natural with children—his usually excitable temperament placid and protective with Mac.

But Rocky was not as much of a natural with children as Ross had turned out to be.

'I know you do,' Ross replied. 'I think he

loves you too,' he added, the roughness in his voice making Carmel's eyes sting.

Ross loved his son. And Mac absolutely adored his father.

The weight on her chest grew as she thought back over the events of the past week. Which had been easy in some ways and incredibly hard in others.

Ross had thrown himself into fatherhood with a determination and purpose—and a hands-on approach—she hadn't expected, but she realised now, she should have.

He was a pragmatic, goal-oriented man, who knew how to pay attention to details. From the moment they'd arrived at the estate, the morning before Conall and Katie were due to fly in to drop Mac off, Carmel had known she had made the right choice to take this extra week and the opportunities it held... To finally give her son a father, however painful this week had promised to be for her.

The estate itself had been the first surprise. She'd expected something sleek and stylish and glaringly modern.

Instead, what she'd found was a lovingly restored Italianate mansion—reminiscent of something straight out of *The Great Gatsby*—which had been meticulously prepared for their son's arrival. Not only had Ross had a room re-painted next to hers in the large guest house by the pool, and fitted with everything a little boy could possibly want—including a bed shaped like a pirate ship and a box full of age-appropriate toys—he'd even thought to have the estate's pool fenced in.

The workmen had been finishing off the railings when they had arrived, and he'd simply said, 'I thought it would be best to make sure he couldn't hurt himself.'

At that moment, she'd had to force herself not to allow that foolish bubble of hope to get wedged in her throat again. Not to give into the emotions that had derailed her during their week together in New York.

The interrogation she'd had from Con during his flying visit had helped. Her brother had questioned her about whether there was 'something going on' between them as soon as they'd been alone together after putting Mac to bed. And she'd been able to tell him the truth, or as much of the truth as he deserved to know, that there was nothing going on between them, not any more.

He'd looked at her suspiciously, no doubt picking up on the qualification in the statement, but to her surprise, instead of giving her another earful about how wrong Ross De Courtney was for her—something she was already well aware of—her brother had simply sighed, then given her a hard hug and whispered:

'Be careful, Mel. You and Mac are precious to me—and I don't want to see either one of you hurt.'

Conall's capitulation had empowered her despite the pain. That her brother had finally accepted she had the right to make her own choices felt important, like a validation, that she was doing the right thing now by stepping back, taking stock, instead of rushing headlong into feelings that would never be reciprocated.

The only problem was, knowing she was doing the right thing hadn't made it any easier to deal with the news that Con was about to become a father himself.

She'd been overjoyed for him and Katie, of course she had. She knew he would make a magnificent father and Katie a wonderful mother. But a secret, shameful, mean-spirited part of her had also resented the fact her brother was going to have it all, when she could not.

And as she'd watched Ross begin to establish a strong, loving relationship with their son, that niggling, mean-spirited, resentful part of herself had refused to go away.

Which was of course ludicrous, because the man had surprised her in the best way possible.

He'd talked to Mac so carefully, so practically, and increasingly taken on the more difficult elements of childcare without hesitation—had even, she could admit now, established a rapport with their son that was very different from her own. Where she tended to baby Mac, to worry about the risks rather than see the reward of allowing her son more independence, Ross was firmer with him, but also bolder. He was protective but also pragmatic and she'd been forced to admit that it had allowed Mac to gain in confidence, particularly in the swimming pool, where he'd been tentative at the beginning of the week to put his head under the water, but was now happy to leap in and go under, as long as he knew Ross would be there to scoop him up if he struggled.

She hated that she'd even resented a little bit seeing Mac grow to rely on his father, but she had. Up till now it had only ever been her and Mac. She'd held all the cards, made all the decisions. And while on the one hand it had been good at the end of each day to have someone else to talk to about Mac, it had also been much harder than she had expected to let go of that control. To know that she wasn't the only one who would have a say in Mac's upbringing from now on.

They hadn't had any conversations about visitation rights, formal custody agreements—perhaps because she had been careful to keep the evening meals they shared to an absolute minimum, the torture of being alone with Ross, and knowing she had no right to touch him, to indulge the pulsing ache in her sex as well as her heart, quite hard enough without being forced to talk about the permanent relationship she was going to have to share with him now.

Unfortunately, she doubted Ross would let her get away with that again tonight. She was already dreading the thought of spending the evening talking about the legalities of their continued relationship—in sterile, unemotional detail, when unemotional was the last thing she felt.

'Okay, buster, how about we feed you and the dog?' Ross said as he lifted Mac back into his arms, and the boy wrapped his arm around his neck.

'I want pizza.'

'What? Again?' Ross did a comical double take.

Mac nodded enthusiastically.

Ross laughed. 'I guess we'll have to ask Ellie if she has any left,' he said, talking about the chef who Mac had charmed just like everyone else on the six-person staff.

'Yes, please, Mr Ross,' he said, playing with Ross's hair now, in the way he had always done with her when she held him like that.

Mr Ross.

The name echoed miserably in Carmel's heart. Like a symbol of her cowardice and selfishness in the last six days. It was way past time

Mac knew who Ross really was. Not just Mammy's friend, but his father.

They hadn't had a chance to discuss it in the last six days, like so much else about Ross's permanent relationship with his son, because she'd avoided it. The same way she'd avoided being alone with Mac's daddy.

She swallowed heavily as Ross walked towards her toting their son, the surge of desire at the sight of his long limbs and naked chest prickling across her skin like wildfire—and making her feel like even more of a failure. Even more of a fraud.

Ross had scrupulously observed her request to end their intimate relationship while Mac was here. He'd escorted her to the guest house, after they had their meal together on the nearby terrace each evening. And had made no move to even touch her, let alone kiss her, since they'd arrived at the mansion.

And in a weird way, she'd even resented that too—that it was so easy for him to end their physical relationship, when it was so hard for her.

Her gaze took in the toned skin glistening in the afternoon sunlight, the bunched muscles of his biceps as he held their son aloft, the rakish beard scruff shadowing his jaw, which she'd watched appear in the last few days and had been itching to run her nails through.

Each night she woke from dreams, sweaty and aroused, the longing so intense she'd often had to resort to finding her own release.

The demands of navigating the massive adjustments when it came to co-parenting their child had taken some of the edge off that insistent, endless yearning in the early days, but every time she was near Ross now, she felt the pull. And she knew he felt it too.

She'd seen him watching her, when he thought she wasn't looking.

But what was worse, she couldn't seem to separate the physical yearning from the emotional yearning any more. Instead of their enforced abstinence making it go away, it seemed to have made it gather and grow, to become this huge lump of need and longing.

'I'm going to take Mac in now. He wants pizza again, is that okay?' Ross stood before her in all his glory, the prickles of heat now both damning her and terrifying her.

'Please, Mammy, can I now?' Mac chimed in.

'I don't suppose another pizza night would do any harm,' she said.

Mac started cheering.

'Cool,' Ross said, his voice roughening as his gaze flicked to her cleavage and back up again. 'You want me to handle his bath and bedtime routine?' he asked.

'Why don't we do it together?' she said. She

should tell Mac Ross was his daddy. What was she waiting for? This wasn't about her and Ross, and it never had been. Perhaps if she finally acknowledged that—told her little boy who Ross really was—it would make the craving shrink, instead of grow.

He nodded and headed off with their baby in his arms, Rocky following on their heels.

Her gaze dipped to admire his glutes in the wet shorts. She forced it back up.

Focus, Mel, on what's best for Mac. And only Mac.

'Mammy, Mammy, Mr Ross said if Rocky has a puppy we can have him. Can we?'

Ross watched Mac reach out from his bed as his mother walked into the little boy's bedroom.

'Oh, did he now?' she said as she perched on the edge of the bed and gave their son an easy hug. She sent Ross a tense smile, and he caught a whiff of her scent—earthy and hopelessly seductive—the surge of need shot through him, vicious, unstoppable and unrelenting.

Only one more night to keep your hands to yourself.

They'd managed to stick to their no-sex rule, had focussed on their son these past few days—he couldn't afford to give into the need now. He dragged his gaze away from her to concentrate on the boy.

'It's okay, I doubt Rocky will be having pups any time soon,' he said, determined to keep his mind on what mattered, instead of what shouldn't.

The last six days had been a revelation in so many ways. He had fallen completely and utterly under the spell of the little boy who he still couldn't quite believe was a part of him. And fatherhood, much to his astonishment, hadn't been nearly as much of a struggle as he'd assumed. It was intense and disturbing on one level, the emotional independence he'd clung to for so long now utterly shot to hell. Every time he held the child's soft, sturdy body in his arms, listened to him giggle, or even whine, watched his small round face light up with excitement or frown with intelligence, or breathed in the scent of talcum powder and bubblegum shampoo, the fierceness of what he felt still shocked him, but it didn't terrify him any more.

His feelings about Mac were surprisingly simple and straightforward and, once he'd let them in without hesitation, were much easier to handle than to deny… His feelings for the boy's mother, though, remained a minefield that had only got worse as the week wore on.

Especially as he watched her struggle with the new reality of letting him be a father to her son.

He wanted her incessantly, of course. The effort to stay away from her, not to let their quiet evening meals lead to more, had been pure torture. But far worse was the yearning, the desire to be with her constantly, the fascination of simply watching her. It made him feel like the small boy he'd once been, giving ownership of his happiness to someone else.

But it was that struggle to share her son, the moments when he could see the doubts and fears cross her face, and realised how hard she must have had to strive to do this all alone, that had really crucified him.

Because it had made him realise how strong and how brave she really was.

The nightmares, not surprisingly, now he could no longer hold her in his arms each night, had also come back with a vengeance. Haunting his dreams and waking him up, confused, alone and yet painfully aroused.

'Can we have a puppy, Mammy, please?' Mac held her cheeks, forcing her to look directly at him.

Ross huffed out a laugh, trying to ease the tension in his gut. And force the sweet, simple feelings for the child to the fore. Because they made so much more sense than his obsession with Carmel.

'Mr Ross said so. Can we?'

Carmel tugged her face away and laughed. The first real laugh he'd heard from her in days.

The light musical sound arrowed into Ross's gut, as it always did.

'We'll see, but before you go to sleep, I have something important to tell you,' she said, deflecting the boy's attention with an ease that always impressed him. 'Or rather, *we* have something important to tell you,' she said, glancing his way and sending him a look that made his heart thunder even harder.

He frowned, confused by the direction of the conversation, and the fierce glow in her eyes... He'd seen it before, on the pool terrace that afternoon, and so many other times in the past few days, often when he was with Mac. It disturbed him how it only increased the yearning.

She's not yours...she can't be...you don't want her to be.

'What, Mammy?' Mac said at the exact same time as he asked.

'We do?'

She nodded at him, then turned back to their son, but her hand reached out and covered his on the bedspread. The touch was electric, sparking so many reactions, not one of them safe, or subtle, or secure.

'Do you remember, you once asked me why you didn't have a daddy, Mac?' she said.

Mac nodded as Ross's heart began to pound painfully. Was she about to tell the boy who he really was? Damn it, he wasn't prepared for this.

'You said I did, but he couldn't be with me,' the little boy said as the pain in Ross's chest twisted with guilt, his grip on his emotions slipping even further.

Carmel nodded. So calm, when he could feel himself falling apart inside.

'He's with us now. Mr Ross is your father, Mac. And he wants to be a part of your life now, very much.'

Mac blinked sleepily, then his eyes widened, the spark of joy and instant acceptance making Ross's heart slam against his rib in hard heavy thumps.

'Really?' he asked, his little brows launching up his forehead.

Ross leaned forward, his hand shaking as he cupped his son's cheek. The boy's skin felt warm and impossibly soft beneath his palm. 'Yes, really,' he confirmed, his words coming out on a husky breath, the emotion all but choking him now.

'I'm sorry I wasn't here sooner,' he said, trying to concentrate on the child, and not the fissure opening up in his chest.

The boy was a smart, sweet, bright, brilliant child—who loved dogs and playing in the pool, who could eat a whole slice of pizza without taking a breath, and charm the pants off everyone he met—and he couldn't have been prouder to be his father. So why did he feel as if the black hole were opening up to swallow him whole?

'Can I call you Daddy?' the little boy asked, looking hesitant for the first time since Ross had met him.

'Of course, I would love for you to call me Daddy,' he replied. 'If you want to,' he finished, as it occurred to him he'd never called his own father by such a familiar name.

As much as he hated to think of the man who had frightened him so much as a child, and whom he had despised as an adult, he clung to that distinction.

Carmel had told him once his own father's failings as a human being didn't have to be his failings, and she'd been right about that. He would strive now to earn this child's trust and respect, the way his own father had never earned his.

But as the little boy flung his arms around his neck and whispered into his ear, 'Daddy, don't forget now, I want a puppy,' the aching hole in his heart refused to go away.

He blinked, the stinging sensation in his eyes making the hole bigger as he lifted the child out of his arms and placed him back in the bed.

'We'll have to talk about that more with your mother, and Rocky, but your request has been duly noted,' he said, the words scraping against his larynx. 'I think it's time for you to go to sleep now. You have a long journey home to-morrow,' he added, the thought crucifying him even more.

But as he pulled away, to let Carmel finish tucking their son in, the word *home* echoed in his chest and seemed to scrape against his throat.

The thought of how much he was going to miss his son, how much he was going to miss them both once they were gone tomorrow, only compounded the sense of loss, of pain and con-fusion.

He'd thought about it, of course he had, but until this moment he hadn't realised that they had turned this huge, palatial estate into a home in the last week. The way Carmel had turned his loft in Tribeca into a home too. The thought terrified him.

How had he let that happen? When had he ever been anything but self-sufficient? How come it only made him feel emptier inside?

Ross lifted off the bed, his steps heavy as he walked to the door, to give Carmel time to set-tle the boy, but then he heard the small sleepy voice say, 'Goodnight, Daddy.'

'Goodnight, son,' he replied.

He left the guest house and walked out onto the lawn beside the pool terrace to relieve the choking sensation in his throat. He looked up at the stars, and felt the deep sense of loss at the thought of returning to the city tomorrow. Without them.

He had to get out of here, to get away, from the pain in his chest and the hole she had made in his heart.

Resentment flared. She shouldn't have told Mac like that. Without his input. Shouldn't have hijacked him.

He spotted Rocky sleeping on one of the loungers, headed towards the small gate into the pool area ready to take the dog back to the main house, when he heard the guest house's door open behind him.

Longing shot through him. Swiftly followed by anger. Because the black hole in his stomach remained, which he had no idea how to repair now.

He turned, to see her walking towards him, the summery dress she'd changed into fluttering around her legs in the evening breeze. She had the baby monitor in her hand, which she always brought with her when they ate out on the garden terrace in view of the guest house.

'Why did you tell him?' he said, making no effort to keep the brittle edge of anger out of his voice—to disguise all the other emotions churning in his gut, which he had no idea now how to control… Longing, need, desire and a fear so huge it all but consumed him.

'I thought it was past time,' she said, with a flippancy that infuriated him even more.

How was this so easy for her?

'You don't think we should have talked about it first?' he said, still trying to control the brutal turmoil she had triggered.

She tilted her head to one side, considering, her whole face suffused by that ethereal glow that had captivated him and terrified him. *Always.* Ever since that sultry summer night so long ago when she'd mesmerised him with her soft lilting accent, her smart, erudite and impulsive personality and the rich scent of her arousal. She was looking at him now the way she'd looked at him then, as if she saw right through him. Knew all the things about him he didn't want her to know. Could see the frightened boy he'd once been, inside the man.

Exposed was too small a word for how it made him feel.

Exposed, and wary and… Needy. Damn it.

'I suppose,' she said. 'But we've only this one more night together, so I saw no point in waiting.'

We've only this one more night together.

The yearning reverberated through him, twisting something deep inside. Yanking at that empty space that had been growing ever since he'd seen her again… And he was very much afraid only she would ever fill.

The desire surged through him again, but this time it was sure and solid and elemental. And simple, unlike all the thoughts and feelings queuing up in his throat.

He stepped towards her, not sure what he was doing any more, but knowing he needed to taste her again, just once more. This enforced celibacy had been her idea, but he'd embraced it after his conversation with Katie, believing it was the best way, hell, the only way, to create the distance he needed to let her go...

But somehow it had backfired on him—because not having her had only made him want her more.

'Don't tempt me, Carmel,' he murmured, seeing her ragged pulse punch her collarbone and hearing the shattered pants of her breathing. She felt it too, this hunger, this need. That was all this was, a physical connection so intense they'd only increased it by keeping their hands to themselves... 'I'm not in the mood,' he finished, the statement closer to the truth than he wanted it to be.

He was on edge, the emotions he didn't understand, for her as much as the child, too close to the surface, threatening to tip him over into the abyss.

He heard the shattered sigh, felt her hands brace against his waist, saw her gaze darken with awareness... He braced himself, expecting her to pull back, even as her spicy scent filled his nostrils and the desire, so fierce, so urgent, beat in his groin.

But instead, she lifted her chin, the challenge in her gaze unmistakable as her fingers fisted in his shirt, the stars reflected in her eyes bottomless enough to drown him as she leaned into him.

'Kiss me, Ross,' she whispered, bold, provocative and as tortured as he was. 'We've only this one night, why should we waste it?'

His control snapped, like a high-tension wire winched too tightly.

He thrust his fingers into her hair, tugged her head back and slanted his mouth across hers, capturing her sigh of surrender and plunging his tongue deep into her mouth.

He took command of the kiss, absorbing her sighs, dragging her into his arms, grinding the hard weight of his arousal against her sex. Forcing back the turmoil of emotions lodged in his gut at the thought that he had to let her go tomorrow.

With the knowledge that, tonight, she was all his.

Heat spread through her body like wildfire, but it was the emotion closing her throat that made her groan as Ross's tongue invaded her mouth, claiming her sighs for the first time in six days.

She tried to focus on the need, that brutal endorphin rush, but the terrible truth kept echoing in her brain.

You're not just falling, you've fallen. This man is it for you. There's no going back now. There never was.

His hands cupped her bottom, pressing her against the prominent ridge of his arousal, letting her know how much he needed her, how much he wanted her too. Clasping her waist, he lifted her easily into his arms, and wrenched his mouth away. She missed it instantly, the longing already at fever pitch.

'Where?' he rasped.

'My room,' she gasped. 'But we'll have to be quiet.' She'd dropped the baby monitor in the grass. But they would hear Mac if he woke up.

'Quiet? Yeah…' he said, his lips doing diabolical things to her neck, and her heart rate.

'Mammy? I had a bad dream.'

Mac's cry didn't register at first through the fog of dazed heat and terrifying emotion, until Ross froze, his fingers digging into her hips. His head jerked up and she saw the stricken look in his eyes before he gasped. 'Oh, God.'

He put her down so suddenly she stumbled. Looking over her shoulder, she saw Mac standing in the doorway of the guest house, in his PJs, his hair rumpled, rubbing his eyes.

The flames that had been burning in her abdomen died down as she tried to switch into mummy mode. The heat continued to burn in her cheeks, though, as she scooped up their son. 'It's okay, baby. Mammy's here.'

Her little boy wrapped his arms round her neck, snuggled his face into her shoulder, still mostly asleep, thank goodness. She couldn't help the pounding in her chest as she carted him back to bed and tucked him in—getting a sleepy rendition of his nightmare, which had involved an enormous pizza and a puppy who kept eating Mac's share.

After kissing him, and promising that when they got a puppy they'd make sure it didn't like pizza, she levered herself off the bed.

Mac was already asleep as she rechecked the room's monitor, giving herself time before she returned outside.

What had they just been about to do? Because it had been so much more than just the fever of desire.

'I love him.'

She whispered the words to herself, forcing herself to face them, knowing them to be true, despite the fear still gripping her chest.

She closed the door to her little boy's room, stood with her back to it and tried to focus. She'd tried to deny her feelings for Ross, for six days, maybe even longer than that. Tried to make this need, this connection, about nothing but sex and her own insecurities. She'd been so scared before, terrified even, of admitting the truth to herself.

But how could it be so wrong? He'd shown himself to be a good father, a good man in the last week. She'd come to know him for who he really was. He wasn't the man she'd fallen for that night four years ago. Not a romantic notion, but flesh and blood, with fears and insecurities just like hers. He could make mistakes, try and fail, just as she had, but she admired him for that now. And yes, there were many things he seemed incapable or unwilling to share, about his past, his childhood, but she knew he had struggled to overcome them. Surely that was what mattered now.

How could she know how Ross really felt about her, about them, about the chance for them to make a future together with their son, instead of apart, if she didn't tell him she loved him? Her fear of her feelings had never really been about Ross and her—it had simply been an echo of that little girl. Who had become so scared to fail she'd refused to try.

She took a deep breath, the fear still huge, but somehow not as black or impenetrable. Not as final. Because now, finally, she had a plan.

She walked back out of the guest house to see Ross standing with his back to her. Her heart did a giddy two-step, the emotion flooding her again.

God, he was so gorgeous, so hot, but he was also flawed, and human, just as she was.

He held the dropped monitor in his hand, the rigid set of his shoulders reminding her of the haunted, horrified look that had crossed his face when he had spotted Mac.

Her courage faltered a little as she approached him. With his head bowed, and his body radiating tension, he seemed a million miles away. What had caused that awful look? she wondered.

She touched his shoulder and he jerked. 'It's okay, Daddy,' she murmured as he turned towards her. 'We didn't scar him for life,' she added, trying to keep her voice light and even, and ignore the painful hope swelling in her chest.

'Ross, what's wrong?' she said when she got a look at his face.

Where was the man who had been devouring her moments ago with such urgency? The man she was finally ready to admit she loved? Because the man in front of her now looked like a ghost. The blank expression so rigid, it was starting to scare her.

'Nothing,' he murmured, his voice as controlled as the rest of him. 'I'm tired. And I'm sure you are too,' he said. 'I'll have the staff bring some food over for you. You've got a long day tomorrow—and I need to head back to Manhattan early. I'll be over in the morning to say goodbye to Mac.'

She'd barely absorbed the long list of details—which he must have been preparing while she was putting Mac back to bed—before he nodded and turned.

Everything inside her rebelled.

No.

She grasped his arm to stop him walking away. 'Wait. What? That's it?'

She could feel the frantic beat of her heart threatening to choke her. But ignored it. This couldn't be happening. How could he suddenly be so cold? When only moments before…?

His mildly puzzled frown—so distant, so vacant—made the pain in her chest increase. 'I think it's for the best we don't finish what we started—which would clearly have been a mistake.'

'A…a mistake?' she stuttered, still stunned by the sudden change in him from wild, passionate lover to cold robot. 'How can it be a mistake when I… I'm in love with you?'

The declaration burst out on a tortured breath. It wasn't how she'd planned to tell him. But that sudden dismissal had left her reeling. Frantic and scared and suddenly so unsure again.

She'd never been a person to temper her feelings. To judge and weigh all the pros and cons carefully, methodically, before making a move. She'd seen that impulsiveness as a weakness for so long. Something to be corrected and suppressed. But she didn't want to live like that any more. To try and deny rather than confront. She was sick of being a coward.

If she'd been wrong, about everything she thought had been happening between them, about where they might go from here, she needed to know now. She could deal with the worst, she told herself. She just couldn't deal with lying to herself any longer.

He blinked several times, clearly as shocked as she was by the whispered revelation. But then a muscle in his jaw tensed, and the first stirrings of nausea churned in her stomach, alongside a deep wave of sadness. The same sadness that had overwhelmed her once before, when she'd received that cold, cruel, cutting text. How could she have forgotten that feeling so easily? Enough to open herself to the same torment again?

'You don't love me, Carmel. What you feel for me is infatuation, believe me, it will pass.'

No, it won't, and I don't want it to. Why can't we be a family? Why can't you let me in?

It was what she wanted to say, what she wanted to shout at him so he would hear her. Her feelings were her own and he had no right to doubt them… But the sadness had spread like a black cloud, over the bright twinkle of hope, covering everything in a thick impenetrable shadow and she knew... This wasn't her decision, it was his. She couldn't make him love her, any more than she had been able to make her mother love her.

And it would only hurt her more to try.

When she fell in love it was fierce and true and she was very much afraid for ever. But she was also a realist. And what she had to do now was deal with the truth. Because if he couldn't love her back, couldn't even accept her feelings for him, what chance would they ever have?

So she said nothing, just stood dumbly, refusing to fight, refusing to cry, but most of all refusing to beg, as he walked into the night.

And the next day, when he came to the guest house to say goodbye to his son, she applied her make-up carefully so he wouldn't see the tears she'd shed over him. And she forced herself to stay strong, to stay calm, to say nothing about the agony of longing and to focus on keeping things light and upbeat for their little boy.

She told herself she would get over it. And she forced herself to pack away all her half-formed dreams for them the same way she packed away her clothes.

But when they boarded the De Courtney Corp chopper at the estate's heliport and she watched Ross standing on the grass and waving goodbye, his dark hair flattened by the wind from the helicopter's blades, the beard scruff that had abraded her skin the night before during that ferocious kiss now shaved off, she held her little boy a bit too tightly, and knew it was going to take a lot more than expertly applied make-up to repair her shattered heart.

CHAPTER FOURTEEN

'MR DE COURTNEY, the conference video call with the European hub is due to start in five minutes.'

Ross stared aimlessly at the Manhattan skyline from his office at the top of De Courtney Corp's US headquarters, only vaguely aware of his assistant's voice, so exhausted he wasn't sure he even had the energy to switch on his computer, let alone conduct a two-hour video call. It was three days, three long days since he had left Long Island, since he had watched the chopper containing Carmel and his son disappear on the horizon, and he still couldn't get her face out of his mind. Or the words she'd whispered to him:

'I'm in love with you.'

But the surge of impossible hope that replaying those words in his mind over and over again brought with it faded into a morass of guilt and loathing, and horror, as he recalled the sight of his child, his son, so small, so vulnerable, witnessing that frantic kiss. And the terrible memories that sight had triggered, memories he had buried for so long, memories he had only ever grasped in nightmares until three days ago, had come slamming back into his consciousness ever since… And refused to leave him now.

The sick dread pressed against his throat again.

His father's voice cold, callous, cruel, his mother's pleading, the cries, the agony, the blood…

He thrust shaking fingers through his hair.

How could Carmel love him when he was only half a man? And that half was not that different from his own father after all…

'Would you like me to get you some coffee before you start, Mr De Courtney?'

'No,' he said, turning to see his personal assistant standing at the door, looking concerned. 'Actually, yes, but can you cancel the call, Daniel?' he said.

'Um…of course…certainly, sir,' the young man said, but he looked even more concerned and completely confused. Probably because Ross had never shirked a work responsibility in his life.

He turned back to the view he couldn't see as his PA left to get his coffee.

He couldn't go on like this. He needed help. He felt as if he were in a fog, a dark, cloying fog he would never find his way out of. Mostly, he

his own voice as her familiar face appeared
on the screen.

'Ross, what on earth did you do?'

The forthright, even aggressive tone was so
unlike his usually sweet and malleable sister, all
he could do was blink. 'What?'

'To Carmel, you dolt?'

The mention of her name had the pain he
had been keeping so carefully leashed charging through his system all over again.

'You've seen her? What's wrong with her?
Is she sick?' he said, concern and panic taking
hold and shaking him to his core.

'We spoke to her via video chat, last night.
And yes, she's sick. Heartsick. Although...' Her
eyes narrowed. 'Ross, you look even worse than
she does. What happened between you two?'
The soft concern in her voice made the guilt
bloom like a mushroom cloud.

He swallowed convulsively, to control the
new wave of nausea. 'She told me she loved me
and I threw it back in her face,' he said, blurting
out the truth. But he was past caring now, what
Katie thought of him, what anyone thought of
im. 'I want to fix it, but I don't know if I can.'

'Oh, Ross. Of course you can, if you want
enough,' Katie said, the concern in her gaze
ning to determination. 'Do you?' she asked.

Yes, yes, I do,' he said—that much at least
simple. 'But I've made such a mess of ev-

needed Carmel. She was the light on th
zon, thoughts of her the only thing he se
to be able to cling onto when those dark m
ories loomed.

But he also couldn't forget her shattered ex
pression that night, and her listless behaviour the
next morning. So calm, so controlled, so devoid
of passion. And so unlike the woman he knew.

He'd done that to her. How could he ask her
for help, when his knee-jerk reaction to her declaration of love had destroyed everything they
might have had?

'Mr De Courtney, you have a video caller,'
Daniel said, walking back into the office with
a cup of coffee. 'A Mrs O'Riordan?'

Carmel? The brutal surge of adrenaline was
painfully dispelled when Daniel added, 'She
says she's your sister?'

Not Carmel, Katie.

But then a strange thing happened. The ru
of need would have disturbed him three d
ago, but he was too exhausted to resist it
Or question it. 'Put her through to my mo
he said, his voice rough.

Maybe Katie would know what he co
how to fix what was broken?

He scraped his fingers through hi
down at his desk, and picked up his s
to click on the link his PA had sent

'Katie?' he said, shamed by the

erything.' He wanted to believe Katie, but how could he vanquish the demons from his childhood? After all this time? And how could he risk sullying Carmel with them? 'But I'm not sure it can be fixed. I'm not even sure I deserve to have it fixed. I certainly know I do not deserve Carmel.'

Katie stared at him. 'You do know that's nonsense, don't you?' she said, the matter-of-fact tone, and her undying faith in him, making him wonder why he had ever believed he didn't want a sister. Or need one.

Then she added with complete conviction. 'I'm sure between the two of us, we can figure out a way to fix it.'

He wasn't sure he believed her, but he knew that if nothing else Katie had given him the courage to try.

CHAPTER FIFTEEN

CARMEL STARED UP at the large detached mansion house tucked at the end of a blossom-strewn mews in London's Kensington as the chauffeur-driven limousine that had picked her up at Heathrow glided through iron gates and into a pebbled courtyard.

'Where are we?' she asked the driver as he opened the door, confused now as well as wary. But too tired to summon the anger that had fortified her during the flight from Galway in Ross's private jet, after the text she'd received two days ago. His personal assistant had requested that she attend a meeting with his legal team today in London—to discuss Mr De Courtney's visitation rights and other financial matters.

Ross hadn't contacted her himself, and that had hurt, at first. But then she had been grateful. Seeing him again would only draw out the agony, she thought miserably as she stepped out of the car. Was that why he hadn't mentioned this meeting when he was video calling Mac last Sunday from Manhattan? Their conversation had been short and stilted and... Well, agonising... Which surely proved it would have been too soon to see him again in the flesh.

'This is one of the De Courtneys' ancestral homes, I believe, Ms O'Riordan,' the chauffeur remarked, although he seemed unsure.

Strange. She had assumed she would meet with Ross's legal team in the company's London headquarters.

'Okay,' she said, forcing down the new wave of sadness. She didn't really want to spend time in his ancestral home, but she followed the driver up the steps to the imposing Georgian building without complaint.

She just wanted to get this over with.

She hadn't slept properly in close to two weeks. Ever since she and Mac had returned from New York. She'd been burying herself in work, and childcare, her go-to strategy when anything in her life was stressing her out. But it seemed this crisis was bigger than any she'd faced before.

Why couldn't she forget that last night, the hope she'd had—so quickly dashed—that she and Ross might build a family together? A future? It had always been a ludicrous pipe dream—one last hurrah for that starstruck girl who had fallen under his spell in an apple orchard a lifetime ago. She needed to pull herself together now and stop thinking about what might have been and instead face the reality... And concentrate on the callous ease with which he had rejected her again.

Mac was what mattered now, and on that subject at least, she knew they were in accord—because she'd heard her son's giggles from the other room as he had chatted with his father in Manhattan for over an hour on Sunday. There was no reason to believe the legal team were going to ambush her with any conditions she couldn't accept. And if they did, she had Con's number on speed dial.

She stepped into the musty interior of the house and shivered. The gloomy hallway, mostly devoid of furniture, was even more austere and forbidding than the outside, despite the sunlight coming in through the stained-glass window above the door and illuminating the dust motes in the stale air.

The chauffeur stood back to let her enter then pointed towards an open door at the end of the hallway. 'I was asked to direct you to the library, and then leave. But I will wait outside for you when you wish to depart.'

Huh?

'Okay.' Carmel frowned, the house's chilling stillness only broken by the loud ticking of an antique grandfather clock as the chauffeur closed the front door behind him.

She made her way down the hallway, the blip of irritation fortifying her. Seriously? Didn't they think she had better things to be doing than spending the day in an empty house?

She stepped into the library. And her heart stopped, then rammed into her throat. Instead of the team of solicitors she had been prepared for, there was only one man, silhouetted in the room's mullioned windows. A man who had delighted and devastated her in equal measure.

'Ross?' she whispered.

Was she dreaming now?

But then he turned from his contemplation of the house's overgrown gardens. And her battered heart threatened to choke her. Pain shot through her, as fresh and raw and real as it had been two weeks ago, and she recalled every single word of his rejection for the five thousandth time.

'You don't love me, Carmel. What you feel for me is infatuation, believe me, it will pass.'

If this was infatuation, she wanted no part of it any more.

'Carmel,' he said, his voice husky and strangely hesitant as he crossed the room's parquet flooring, his footsteps echoing in the empty room—the books that must once have been here long gone.

'What are you doing in London?' she asked, surprised her voice sounded so steady when her ribs had become a vice, squeezing her chest so tightly she was afraid her heart might burst.

She drank in the sight of him, but everything about him now seemed intimidating—his long legs, broad shoulders, that devastatingly handsome face, the planes and angles sharper than she remembered them, the waves of chestnut hair furrowed into haphazard rows, the dark business suit and white shirt, so unlike the man who had played with their son for hours in the pool.

She stepped back, and he stopped.

'Don't, don't come any closer,' she said, the inevitable surge of heat her enemy now, like the painful yearning in her heart. 'If you've brought me here just to tell me again you don't love me, I got the message the first time,' she said, brutally ashamed of the quiver in her voice.

Her eyes stung. She'd shed so many tears for him already, how could there still be more? God, could he not even leave her with this last scrap of dignity?

'I brought you here to show you the house where I grew up.' He glanced around the room, thrusting his hands into his pockets, the hunched shoulders matching the flash of pain and loathing she had seen that night.

She should tell him no, she wasn't interested any more. But she couldn't seem to get the words out, past the thunderous emotion still choking her.

'Why?' she managed to ask, suddenly unbearably weary. Unbearably tense. The struggle to hold onto her tears so hard.

'Because I want you to know everything. So you can understand what happened on our last night, when you told me you loved me.'

She frowned. What was this now? Did he want her to say it again? So he could reject her again? Why was he talking in riddles?

But even as the caustic thoughts assailed her, she could see that wasn't it. He looked tormented, on edge—whatever ghosts had haunted him that night, this was where they dwelled. And suddenly she wanted to know—all those things he had been so unwilling to share with her. So all she said was, 'Okay.'

He gave a stiff nod, then glanced around the

empty shelves. 'This is the room where my father destroyed the only photograph I had of my mother in front of me,' he said, his voice so flat and remote it was chilling. 'I was seven.'

She shuddered, reminded of how he had spoken to her two weeks ago in that same monotone.

'That's hideous,' she managed. 'Why would he do such a thing?'

He shrugged, the movement tense but somehow painfully resigned too, as if it didn't really matter, when it clearly still hurt.

'He was sending me to boarding school and he was furious that I was still wetting the bed at night, according to my governess. I'd been having night terrors ever since…' He hesitated, swallowed. 'Ever since her death, two years before. He was concerned I would embarrass the De Courtney name at school.' His lips lifted in a rueful smile, but there was no humour in it, only sadness. 'To be fair, it worked. I was more terrified of him than the nightmares.'

'I… I'm so sorry, Ross. He sounds like a terrible father.'

She wanted to go to him, to hold him, to console him, the way she would Mac when he had a nightmare, but she could see the brittle tension, and sense the struggle within him to hold the demons at bay so he could talk about them. So she kept her distance.

She had known his father had scarred him, but had she ever realised to what extent? She'd dismissed that haunted look two weeks ago when Mac had appeared so unexpectedly, too busy wallowing in the rejection that had followed, the desire to tell him how she felt… Why hadn't she asked questions, thought more about what he might be feeling, instead of focussing on her own?

'If it's hard for you to be here, we don't have to stay,' she added. Suddenly wanting to leave this place. Sure, if he was going to reject her again, to tell her this was why he could never love her, she didn't want it to be here.

But he shook his head slowly, the small quirk of his lips somehow devastatingly poignant. 'Don't let me off the hook so easily, Carmel.'

She nodded slowly, realising that, for whatever reason, she had to let him show her the rest.

He led her out of the library, and up the stairs, reaching a large landing, his movements stiff and mechanical and comprehensively lacking his usual grace. He stopped on the threshold of the first room on the left. A huge piece of furniture—from the shape of it under the dustsheet, probably a four-poster bed—stood in the middle of the room. He hesitated, took in a lungful of air, then stepped inside.

'This is where the night terrors came from. This is the room where I watched my mother and her baby die. And where, the therapist believes, nine months before I may have watched him assault her.'

'Oh, God.' Carmel gasped beside him, then pressed her fingers to her lips. Ross tucked his hands into his pockets to stop them shaking.

One lone tear skimmed down her cheek, crucifying him. He could see pity in her gaze as she turned towards him. But more than that he could see compassion.

The nausea in his gut rose in a wave to push into his throat.

The sick, weightless feeling in his stomach reminded him of those moments—between sleep and waking—when he could see it all again so clearly. But he knew he had to keep talking. He owed her this. So he forced himself to channel the advice the therapist he had employed a week ago at Katie's suggestion had given him.

You're not responsible for her death, Ross. But what you saw between your parents would cause a deep trauma for anyone—let alone a five-year-old child—and that's what we need to address.

He needed to tell her the truth, about the baggage he might well carry with him always—and the truth about his heritage, and the legacy he was terribly afraid might lurk inside him.

'She used to like me to sleep with her,' he said. 'I suspect now to stop him visiting her at night. But I can remember one night. I woke and he was there, beside the bed, kissing her, hurting her, she was crying and he wouldn't stop...' He couldn't say any more, the vision terrifying him even now.

'Ross...' She reached out her hand, grasped his fingers, held on. 'Is that why you freaked out, when Mac woke up and saw us kissing that night?' she asked.

'I... I suppose yes. It brought it all back. But...' He hesitated, scared to say the truth out loud. She squeezed his fingers, giving him the courage he so desperately needed to continue. He forced himself to turn, to look at her, to give it to her straight. 'I wanted you so damn much in that moment. I'm not sure I could have stopped, if you'd asked me. She begged him to stop and he wouldn't and I can't bear the thought that I might... That Mac might have witnessed the same depraved—'

'Ross…' She cut him off, pressed a gentle palm to his cheek, to stop the rambling confession. A lone teardrop fell from her lid. 'What Mac witnessed, if he witnessed anything at all, was a kiss between two consenting adults. It's not the same thing at all,' she said so simply it pierced through the fog at last. The feel of her palm stroking his face felt so soft, so warm, soothing the brutal knots in his belly. 'And anyway, you did stop, so fast you almost dropped me,' she said, the humorous quirk of her lips warming the brutal chill that had overcome him the moment he had walked into this room.

But then she added, 'Can you tell me what happened when she died?'

He dipped his head. He didn't want to talk about it. But somehow it was easier now, knowing she didn't blame him, the way he had blamed himself, for his father's sins.

'I wasn't supposed to be in here,' he said. 'No one saw me, they were too busy trying to save her… But her cries had woken me up,' he said, but then the words simply ground to a halt.

'You don't need to tell me,' she said softly beside him. Weirdly, the fact she would let him stop, if he needed to, gave him the courage to carry on.

'I do… I want to,' he said, knowing it wasn't

pity he saw in those stunning blue eyes, but a fierce compassion. 'I want you to know what you'll be dealing with, because… I still have the nightmares. They came back, after I discovered I had a son. And once I couldn't hold you at night. And they've been much worse, since we left Long Island.'

'Why didn't you tell me, Ross?' Her voice broke on his name, another tear slipping down her cheek.

'Because I was so ashamed,' he said simply.

She shook her head, then gripped his wrist and tugged his hand out of his pocket. She threaded her fingers through his and held on. The contact was like a balm again, releasing the renewed pressure in his chest.

'Is that why you had the vasectomy?' she asked, with an emotional intelligence that he now knew he found as captivating as the rest of her.

He nodded. Funny she should figure that out when he never had.

'Yes, I think it was. I guess it all got jumbled up in my mind. He was there, in the room, demanding they save the baby, no matter what. It was another boy, another male heir, and I expect that was why he had assaulted her in the first place. Because that was always his priority. Continuing the De Courtney legacy.' He gathered in a painful breath, let it out again. 'There was so much blood,' he murmured, seeing it all again. The private medical team rushing around, the metallic smell suffocating him, the silent scream tearing a hole in his chest.

His breathing became laboured, but her hand gripped his, reassuring, empowering, making the nightmare vision retreat.

'So you had yourself sterilised as a young man, so you would never put a woman through what he had put your mother through,' she said softly. 'Can't you see how different that makes you from him?'

'Yes,' he said, because finally he did see. But then he dropped his chin, swallowed round the rawness in his own throat. 'Although it's kind of screwed up, especially as I never properly checked to find out if the damn procedure had actually worked.'

'Well, thank goodness it didn't or we wouldn't have Mac,' she said.

He chuckled at the force of feeling in the remark, his relief almost as glorious as the sudden feeling of lightness. The realisation she had lifted a weight that had burdened him for far too long.

He dragged her out of the room, slammed

the door. Feeling strangely empowered at the thought of shutting out that part of his past. It would always be there, he knew that, but there was no reason to believe it could control him any more. Not if he could do this next bit.

'I spoke to Katie ten days ago.' He clasped her cheeks, no longer able to deny the wealth of feeling moving through him. Desperation yes, but also determination, and a strange sort of acceptance. 'I told her everything, and she suggested I get a therapist. I've had a couple of sessions already, and…' He paused, swallowed. 'It may take me a long time to finally get the nightmares to stop.' Although oddly, after this conversation with Carmel, he already felt as if he had turned an important corner.

Identifying your demons was one thing, but defeating them was another, and she had already helped him with that. He'd managed to laugh in a room that had once filled him with terror. Until today, he would never have believed that was even possible.

'I'm so sorry, Ross,' she said. 'I didn't ask what had spooked you that night and I should have. Instead I burdened you with my feelings when you were struggling to handle your own. It was selfish and immature and—'

'Stop.' He pressed his finger to her lips. 'No,

it wasn't, Carmel,' he said. 'You were honest with me.' God, how he hoped that was still how she felt about him. 'And instead of being honest with you, I protected myself. That's not okay.'

'But, Ross…' She began again, grasping his hands, and looking at him with the same glow in her eyes that had captivated and terrified him so much.

And suddenly he knew… She still loved him. She hadn't changed her mind, even knowing the darkness that lurked inside him and might never be vanquished.

He let go of her cheeks and dropped to one knee, taking her hands in his.

'Ross?' She looked stunned. 'What are you doing?'

'What I should have done two weeks ago,' he said, then swallowed down the last of his fear. 'When you told me you loved me.'

'But—' she said.

'Shh, now,' he said, but he grinned. Damn, but he adored the way she always needed to have the last word. But not this time. This time it was his turn to bare his soul. And her turn to listen. 'What I should have said, what I know now was already in my heart, was that I love you, too. And I love our little boy. And I would really like to marry you.'

Her big blue eyes widened even further, her mouth opening, then closing again.

For the second time ever he'd left her speechless. But this time felt so much better than the last.

'I know you will probably want to wait, until I've had a lot more therapy,' he qualified. 'But I'm planning to relocate to Galway—to buy a house near you and Mac so we can begin to—'

'No,' she interrupted him.

No? His heart jumped, stuttered, but before the panic could set in, she continued.

'No, I don't want to wait,' she declared, tugging him up off his knees as his heart soared. 'We've waited long enough. And so has Mac. And no, you don't need to buy a house. Because we already have one that we can share. It's only two bedrooms, but perhaps, if it's too small, we can—'

'Shut up, Carmel,' he groaned, dragging her into his arms, the weight of emotion all but choking him, but in a good way. In the right way. 'I don't care about the house, as long as you and Mac are in it… And Rocky,' he said.

She chuckled. 'And all his puppies.'

'Because then it will be home,' he finished.

Grasping his shoulders, she boosted herself into his arms. He caught her easily as she wrapped her legs around his waist and began kissing his face.

He kissed her back with all the love bursting in his heart, the heat pounding through his veins as fierce and strong as the happiness enveloping him.

She reared back and gripped his cheeks. 'Now please tell me there's another bedroom in this place so we don't have to seal this deal in the hallway.'

He was still laughing as he sank into her a minute later, on the floor.

EPILOGUE

One year later

ROSS HEARD THE crowd hush and then the strains of the wedding march build at the back of Kildaragh's chapel. He imagined the bridal procession beginning to make their way down the aisle, the very same aisle he had marched down twelve months ago to stop a wedding.

Not yet...don't look yet.

He smiled, appreciating the irony—and the glorious swell of anticipation—as the melodic Celtic tune Carmel had chosen for her entrance matched the heavy thuds of his heartbeat.

Twelve months. Twelve long, endless months it had taken to get to this day. Because apparently he and Carmel had very different opinions about what 'not waiting' a moment longer than necessary to get married actually meant. But in a few minutes the waiting would finally be over.

Carmel, of course, had insisted everything

had to be just right. So there'd been the wait for Immy and Donal's baby boy, Ronan, to be born, then another longer wait for Katie and Conall's daughter, Caitlyn, to finally arrive on Christmas Day. Then there had been a new house to build—so he could move his business headquarters here, as well as having room for his family. He'd put up with all the delays with remarkable patience and fortitude. Given that he'd been desperate to make her his wife—legally, officially, in every way that was humanly possible—as soon as she agreed to marry him. In the end, he'd brought Katie in to help plan the wedding and speed things along. But still it had taken one never-ending year to finally get to this day.

'Daddy, Mammy's coming now,' his little boy and best man—who looked particularly grown up with his blond curls slicked back and wearing a miniature wedding suit—announced loudly beside him. Ross smiled despite the nerves and looked down at his son, who had his arm wrapped around the neck of Ross's other best man, or rather his best dog.

'She looks so pretty,' Mac murmured, the awe in his tone making Ross realise he couldn't wait one damn moment longer.

He shifted round. And his thundering heartbeat got wedged in his throat—virtually cutting off his air supply.

Mac is wrong.

With her russet hair perched precariously on her head and threaded through with wild-flowers, the sleek fall of cream silk accentu-ating her slender curves as she headed down the aisle towards him on her brother's arm, and that stunning bone structure, fair skin and pure blue eyes—only made more bewitching by the wisp of lace covering her face—Mac's mammy wasn't just pretty, she was absolutely stunning.

He had to force himself to keep breathing. Stunning, both inside and out.

At last, his bride and her brother reached them.

Katie and Imelda arrived behind them in their maid-of-honour dresses. His sister and his soon-to-be sister-in-law positively beamed with plea-sure while Donal looked on from his spot in the front row, holding little Ronan securely on his lap and guarding a bassinet with the sleeping Caitlyn in it.

Conall presented Carmel's hand to Ross, then stepped back, winking at him. Incredi-ble to think Con and he had actually become friends over the last year—more than friends, brothers—bonding over the chaos of new fatherhood and their shared dismay at exactly how they were supposed to handle the two extremely strong-willed women they'd chosen to share their lives with.

He took Carmel's hand, felt her fingers tremble in his—and suddenly the only thing he could concentrate on was her. She grinned at him, but the power and poignancy of the moment was reflected in her misty sapphire eyes.

He stroked his thumb across the soft skin and grinned back at her as the powerful thought squeezed his chest too. Tonight, they would be a family, in every sense of the word, before God and man.

'About time you showed up,' he murmured.

She gave a low chuckle, which struck him deep in his abdomen. 'Don't you worry, you'll not be getting rid of me or Mac now.'

He smiled back at her, the elation making his heart swell against his ribs. 'Don't *you* worry, I intend to hold you both to that promise, for all eternity.'

She blinked, the happy sheen in her eyes making his own sting.

But then Mac squeezed himself between them both, holding up the band of white gold Ross had given him not ten minutes ago and shouted, 'Can Rocky and me give you the ring now, Daddy?'

And the whole assembly dissolved into laughter.

'I now declare you man and wife. You may kiss your bride, Ross,' Father Meehan finally announced.

Carmel couldn't stop grinning, her heart so buoyant it was all but flying as Ross finally got around to lifting her veil.

Spontaneous applause swelled under the roof of the old chapel. She could hear Mac cheering like a lunatic as his uncle Conall boosted him into his arms, Rocky's excited barking, and a baby wailing—probably poor Caitlyn woken by all the commotion—and feel the confetti fluttering onto her cheeks. But all she could see was the love dancing in Ross's eyes—pure, true, strong, for ever—exactly the way it was dancing in her heart.

He placed callused palms on her warm cheeks, lifted her face to his, and pressed his mouth to hers at last.

She let out a soft sob, the exquisite sensation gathering in her belly nothing compared to the storm of emotion singing in her heart. The kiss went from sweet to carnal as his tongue delved deep, exploring, exploiting and claiming every inch of her as his. She pressed her hands to his waist and kissed him back with the same force and fury, claiming him right back as hers.

The applause, the barking, the shouting and baby cries faded until all she could hear was the sure solid beat of her heart. But then as her brand-new husband pulled away—forced to come up for air—she leaned up on tiptoes, held him close and whispered in his ear. 'By the way, you should know, in about seven and a bit months' time, it'll not just be me and Mac and Rocky you're stuck with for all eternity.'

His eyes popped wide, his hands tightening on her waist as she watched the emotions—emotions he no longer felt the need to hide from her—flicker across his face. Confusion, surprise, shock, awe… And uninhibited joy.

Then he lifted her off her feet, spun her round and threw his head back to add yet more noise to their wild Irish wedding commotion.

Needless to say it took close to another whole eternity to calm down the dog and their son again long enough to tell them the good news, too.

* * * * *